THE
GHOST
ROAD

PAT BARKER

THE
GHOST
ROAD

A William Abrahams Book

A DUTTON BOOK

DUTTON
Published by the Penguin Group
Penguin Books USA Inc., 375 Hudson Street, New York, New York 10014, U.S.A.
Penguin Books Ltd, 27 Wrights Lane, London W8 5TZ, England
Penguin Books Australia Ltd, Ringwood, Victoria, Australia
Penguin Books Canada Ltd, 10 Alcorn Avenue, Toronto, Ontario, Canada M4V 3B2
Penguin Books (N.Z.) Ltd, 182–190 Wairau Road, Auckland 10, New Zealand

Penguin Books Ltd, Registered Offices: Harmondsworth, Middlesex, England

Published by Dutton, an imprint of Dutton Signet,
a division of Penguin Books USA Inc.
Previously published in Great Britain
by Penguin Books Ltd.

First Dutton Printing, November, 1995
10 9 8 7 6 5 4 3 2 1

ISBN 0-525-94191-6

CIP data is available.

Printed in the United States of America

PUBLISHER'S NOTE
This is a work of fiction. Names, characters, places, and incidents either are the
products of the author's imagination or are used fictitiously, and any resemblance
to actual persons, living or dead, events, or locales is entirely coincidental.

This book is printed on acid-free paper. ∞

For David

Now all roads lead to France
And heavy is the tread
Of the living; but the dead
Returning lightly dance

'Roads', Edward Thomas

PART ONE

ONE

In deck-chairs all along the front the bald pink knees of Bradford businessmen nuzzled the sun. Billy Prior leant on the sea-wall. Ten or twelve feet below him a family was gathering its things together for the trek back to boarding-house or railway station. A fat, middle-aged woman, swollen feet bulging over lace-up shoes, a man with a lobster-coloured tonsure – my God, he'd be regretting it tomorrow – and a small child, a boy, being towelled dry by a young woman. His little tassel wobbled as he stood, square-mouthed with pain, howling, 'Ma-a-am.' Wet sand was the problem. It always was, Prior remembered. However carefully you tiptoed back from that final paddle, your legs got coated all over again, and the towel always hurt.

The child wriggled and his mother slapped him hard, leaving red prints on his chubby buttocks. He stopped screaming, gulped with shock, then settled down to a persistent grizzle. The older woman

protested, 'Hey, our Louie, there's no need for that.'
She grabbed the towel. 'C'mon, give it here, you've
no bloody patience, you.'

The girl – but she was not a girl, she was a woman
of twenty-five or twenty-six, perhaps – retreated,
resentful but also relieved. You could see her problem. Married, but the war, whether by widowing
her or simply by taking her husband away, had
reduced her to a position of tutelage in her mother's
house, and then what was the point? Hot spunk
trickling down the thigh, the months of heaviness,
the child born on a gush of blood – if all that didn't
entitle you to the status and independence of a
woman, what did? Oh, and she'd be frustrated too.
Her old single bed back, or perhaps a double bed
with the child, listening to snores and creaks and farts
from her parents' bed on the other side of the wall.

She was scrabbling in her handbag, dislodging bus
tickets, comb, purse, producing, finally, a packet of
Woodbines. She let the cigarette dangle wetly from
her lower lip while she groped for the matches. Her
lips were plump, a pale salmon pink at the centre,
darkening to brownish red at the edges. She glanced
up, caught him looking at her, and flushed, not with
pleasure – his lust was too blatant to be flattering –
but drawn by it, nevertheless, into the memory of
her unencumbered girlhood.

Her mother was helping the little boy step into his
drawers, his hand a dimpled starfish on her broad
shoulder. The flare of the match caught her attention.

4

'For God's sake, Louie,' she snapped. 'If you could only see how common you look . . .'

Louie's gaze hadn't moved. Her mother turned and squinted up into the sun, seeing the characteristic silhouette that said 'officer'. 'Look for the thin knees,' German snipers were told, but where they saw prey this woman saw a predator. If he'd been a private she'd have asked him what the bloody hell he thought he was gawping at. As it was, she said, 'Nice weather we're having, sir.'

Prior smiled, amused, recognizing his mother's speech, the accent of working-class gentility. 'Let's hope it lasts.'

He touched his cap and withdrew, thinking, as he strolled off, that the girl was neither a widow nor married. The way the mother's voice had cracked with panic over that word 'common' said it all. Louie's knees were by no means glued together, even after the child. And her mother was absolutely right, with that fag stuck in her mouth she did look common. Gloriously, devastatingly, *fuckably* common.

He ought to be getting back to barracks. He had his medical in less than an hour, and it certainly wouldn't do to arrive gasping. He had no business to be drifting along the front looking at girls. But he looked anyway, hoarding golden fuzz on a bare arm, the bluish shadow between breasts thrust together by stays, breathing in lavender sharpened by sweat.

The blare of music inside the fairground drew him

to stand in the entrance. So far today the only young men he'd seen had been in uniform, but here were men as young as himself in civilian dress. Munitions workers. One of them was chatting to a young girl with bright yellow skin. He felt the automatic flow of bile begin and turned away, forcing himself to contemplate the bald grass. A child, holding a stick of candy-floss, turned to watch him, attracted to the man who stood so still among all the swirl and dazzle. He caught her looking at him and smiled, remembering the soft cotton-wool sweetness of candy-floss that turned to clag on the roof of your mouth. She bridled and turned away, clutching her mother's skirt. Very wise.

As he walked on, his smile faded. *He* could have been a munitions worker, he thought. Kept out of danger. Lined his pockets. His father would have wangled him a place in a nice safe reserved occupation, and would not have despised him for it either, unlike many fathers. The weedy little runt would at least have been behaving like a *sensible* weedy little runt, refusing to fight in 'the bosses' war'. But he'd never seriously considered doing that.

Why not? he wondered now. Because I don't want to be one of *them*, he thought, remembering a munitions worker's hand patting a girl's bottom as he helped her into the swing-boat. Not duty, not patriotism, not fear of what other people would think, certainly not that. No, a kind of . . . fastidiousness. Once, as a small boy, he'd slipped chewed-up

6

pieces of fatty mutton into the pocket of his trousers, because he couldn't bring himself to swallow them, and his father, when the crime came to light, had said, in tones of ringing disgust, 'That bairn's too fussy to live.' Too fussy to live, Prior thought. There you are, nowhere near France and an epitaph already. The thought cheered him up enormously.

By now he was walking up the hill towards the barracks, a chest-tightening climb, but he was managing it well. His asthma was good at the moment, better than it had been for months. All the same it might be as well to sit quietly somewhere for a few minutes before he went into the examination room. In the end all he could do was to turn up in a reasonable state, and answer the questions honestly (or at least tell no lies that were likely to be found out). The decision would be taken by other people. It always was.

Though he had managed to take *one* decision himself.

His thoughts shifted to Charles Manning and the last evening they'd spent together in London.

  – *Have you stopped to think what's going to happen if you're not sent back?* Manning had asked. *Six months, at least six months, probably to the end of the war, making sure new recruits wash between their toes.*

  – *Might have its moments.*

  – *Doing a hundred and one completely routine jobs, each of which could be done equally well by somebody else. You'd be much better working at the Ministry. I can't promise to keep the job open.*

– *No, thank you, Charles.*

No, thank you. He was passing the Clarence Gardens Hotel where he'd been stationed briefly last winter before the summons to London came. Plenty of routine jobs there. He and Owen, his fellow nutcase, had arrived on the same day, neither of them welcomed by the CO. They'd been assigned to 'light duties'. Prior became an administrative dogsbody, sorting out the battalion's chaotic filing system. Owen fared yet worse, chivvying the charladies, ordering vegetables, peering into lavatory bowls in search of unmilitary stains. Mitchell had given them hell. Prior got him in the mornings when he was *totally* vile, Owen in the evenings when brandy had mellowed him slightly.

– *What do you expect?* Prior said, when Owen complained. *He's lost two sons. And who shows up instead of them? Couple of twitching Nancy boys from a loony-bin in Scotland.*

Silence from Owen.

– *That's what he thinks, you know.*

As he reached the entrance to the barracks, a squad of men in singlets and shorts, returning from a cross-country run, overtook him and he stood back to let them pass. Bare thighs streaked with mud, steam rising from sweaty chests, glazed eyes, slack mouths, and as they pounded and panted past, he recognized Owen at the head of the column, turning to wave.

★

8

'Good heavens,' Mather said, as Prior pulled off his shirt. 'You haven't been getting much outdoor exercise, have you?'

'I've been working at the Ministry of Munitions.'

Mather was middle aged, furrow-cheeked, sandy-haired, shrewd.

'All right, drop your drawers. Bend over.'

They always went for the arse, Prior thought, doing as he was told. An army marches on its stomach, and hobbles on its haemorrhoids. He felt gloved fingers on his buttocks, separating them, and thought, Better men than you have paid for this.

'I see you've got asthma.'

There? 'Yes, sir.'

'Turn round.'

Another unduly intimate gesture.

'Cough'

Prior cleared his throat.

'I said, *cough.*' The fingers jabbed. 'And again.' The hand changed sides. 'Again.'

Prior was aware of wheezing as he caught his breath.

'How long?'

Prior looked blank, then stammered. 'S-six months, sir.'

'Six months? But it says –'

'I mean, the doctor told my mother I had it when I was six months old, sir.'

'Ah.' Mather turned over a page of the file. 'That makes more sense.'

'Apparently I couldn't tolerate milk.'

Mather looked up. 'Awkward little bugger, weren't you? Well, we'd better have a listen.' He reached for his stethoscope and came towards Prior. 'What were you doing at the Ministry of Munitions?'

'Intelligence, sir.'

'Oooh, *very* impressive. Catch anybody?'

Prior looked bleakly ahead of him. 'Yes.'

'Patrol here caught a German spy on the cliffs.' Mather snorted, fitting the stethoscope. 'Tickled a local yokel with their bayonets more like.'

Prior started to say something, but Mather was listening to his chest. After a few minutes, he straightened up. 'Yes, you have got a bit of a wheeze.' His attention was caught by the scar on Prior's elbow. He turned the arm towards him.

'The Somme,' Prior said.

'Must've hurt.'

'The expression "funny bone" didn't seem appropriate at the time.'

Mather went back to the desk, sat down. 'Now let's see if I've got this straight. You were invalided home with shell-shock. That right? April last year?'

'Yes, sir.'

'And you were sent first to Netley and then to Craiglockhart War Hospital, where you remained till . . . November.' He looked up. 'I suppose you get a lot of dipsomania, in places like that? *Alcohol*, man,' he explained, as Prior continued to look blank.

'Didn't see any, sir. If I had I'd certainly have drunk it.'

'So what *were* your symptoms?'

'I was mute, sir. Some people found it an improvement on the basic model.'

But Mather was reading, not listening. 'W. H. R. Rivers,' he said. 'I knew him. He was two years ahead of me at Bart's. Paralytic stammer.'

Prior looked puzzled. 'No.'

'Ah? Got his own voice back too. He must be good.' He tapped a sheet of paper. 'The discharge report says asthma.'

'I had two attacks while I was there.'

'Hm.' Mather smiled. 'Any problems with the nerves now?'

'No.'

'Appetite?'

'I could eat more than I get.'

'So could we all, laddie. Sleeping all right?'

'Not last night. Bloody tent leaks.'

'Generally?'

'I sleep all right.'

Mather sat back in his chair. 'How did you get in?'

'Through the flap.'

Mather's forefinger shot up. 'Watch it, *laddie*. How did you get into the *army*?'

A brief struggle with temptation, ending as Prior's struggles with temptation usually did. 'I lied to the doctor, Doctor.'

Surprisingly, Mather laughed, a short bark.

'Everybody lied,' Prior said.

'So they did, I remember it well. I saw men who'd climbed out of the window of the workhouse infirmary to come and enlist. Syphilis, epilepsy, tuberculosis, rickets. One lad – little squeaky voice, not a hair on his chin, fourteen, if that – looked me straight in the eye and swore on his mother's life he was nineteen.' Mather smiled, revealing brown teeth. 'Not one of them got past me.'

Oh fuck.

'Gas training,' Mather said.

Silence.

'Well?'

'*Terribly* good idea,' Prior said earnestly.

'Did you go through the huts?'

'No.'

'You must be affected at very low concentrations?'

'I was known as the battalion canary, sir. Partly that. Partly my pleasant, cheerful personality.'

Mather looked at him. 'Get dressed.'

'The point is I managed perfectly well *for three years*. I didn't *once* report sick with asthma *or* the effects of gas.'

'Yes, laddie.' Mather looked unexpectedly compassionate. 'And it might be said you've done your bit.'

A twitch of the pale, proud face. 'Not by me.'

'And the asthma never played you up in France?'

'Never.'

'Two attacks in Craiglockhart. None in France. I wonder why?'

'Open-air life suited my chest, sir.'

'We're not running a sanatorium, laddie. Go on, get dressed. Then you go left along the corridor, turn left at the end, and you'll see a row of chairs. Wait there.'

Mather went into the adjoining room and started on his next victim. Prior dressed, pausing to wipe the sweat off his upper lip. Like going over the top, he thought. No, it wasn't. Nothing was like that. Civilians seemed to use that expression all the time now. I went a bit over the top last night, they said, meaning they'd had a second glass of port. Prior peered into the small looking-glass behind the wash-basin, checking the knot in his tie. If they didn't send him back he was going to be awfully lonely, marooned among civilians with their glib talk. His reflection jeered, *Lonely? You? Oh, c'mon, duckie. You can always split in two.* At least the Board didn't know about *that.* Or rather they didn't, provided Rivers hadn't written to them. A *paralytic* stammer. Not just any old stammer. Paralytic. Interesting, Prior thought, letting himself out of the room.

The place smelled like a barracks. Well, it was a barracks, but the Clarence Gardens Hotel, after months of army use, had not smelled anything like this. His nose twitched, identifying armpits, feet, socks, oil, boot-polish, carbolic soap, the last blown in bubbles between the raw fingers of a boy scrubbing the floor. Rear-end like a truck and a face to match, but Prior produced a charming smile, nevertheless, because he owed it to himself, and strode on, leaving a trail of muddy footprints across the wet floor.

One man waiting. Owen.

'The O's and the P's again,' Owen said, picking up a pile of *John Bulls* from the vacant chair and dumping them on the floor. They'd last waited together like this at Craiglockhart, at their final board.

Prior jerked his head at the door. 'Who's in?'

'Nesbit. He's been in thirty minutes.'

'What's taking so long?'

Owen hesitated, then mouthed, 'Clap.'

Well, Prior thought, that was one way of getting out of it. And then he thought, You uncharitable bastard, how do you know he got it deliberately? And then he thought, Well, I *am* an uncharitable bastard.

'I won't take long,' Owen said. 'I'm GS already.'

'Then why are you here?'

'Irregular heartbeat. I added my name to the draft, but when I had the final medical they promptly took it off again.'

'You added your name to the draft? Sure it's your *heart* that's wrong?'

Owen laughed, and looked away. 'I'd just heard Sassoon was wounded. It seemed the only thing to do.'

Yes, Prior thought, it would. He remembered them at Craiglockhart: the incongruous pair, Sassoon

14

so tall, Owen so short, the love Owen hadn't been able, or hadn't bothered, to disguise.

'*Also*,' Owen said, 'I was getting pretty tired of being regarded as "a twitching Nancy boy from a loony-bin in Scotland".'

Prior smiled. 'I applied it to myself as well.'

Owen had cut himself shaving, he noticed. Blood in shiny brown flakes filled the crease between cheek and earlobe.

'Do you think you'll be all right this time?'

Owen said cheerfully, 'Oh, yes, I should think so. I've been doing a lot of running.'

'I saw.'

The door opened. Nesbit came out, looking distinctly pale.

Owen stood up. 'Do they want me in?'

'I don't know.'

Owen sat down again. 'Worse than the dentist, isn't it?' he said, forcing a laugh.

A few minutes later he was called in. Prior sat listening to the murmur of voices, thinking what bloody awful luck it was to have got Mather. Some MOs would send a corpse back if you propped one up in front of them, particularly now when every man was needed for the latest in a long line of 'one last pushes'. Abruptly, before he was ready, the door opened and Owen came out. Owen started to speak and then, realizing the Board's secretary had followed him, raised a thumb instead. From which Prior concluded that Owen's chances of ending the year deaf, blind, dumb, paralysed, doubly incontinent, insane, brain damaged or − if he were lucky − just plain dead had enormously increased. We're all mad here, he thought, following the secretary into the room, saluting, sitting down in the solitary chair facing the long table, meeting every eye confidently but not *too* confidently. And really, amidst the general insanity, was it fair to penalize a man merely because in conditions of extreme stress he tended to develop two separate personalities? You *could* argue the army was getting a bargain.

After the first few questions he began to relax. They were concentrating on his asthma and the risks of exposure to gas, and to those questions he had one totally convincing answer: he had been out to France three times and on none of these occasions had he been invalided back to base or home to England because of asthma. Trench fever, yes; wound, yes; shell-shock, yes. Asthma, *no*.

When the last question had been asked and answered, Mitchell drew the papers together in front of him, and patted them into shape. Prior watched the big white hands with their sprinkling of age spots and the shadowing of hair at the sides.

'Right,' Mitchell said at last. 'I think that's all . . .'

The pause was so long Prior began to wonder whether he would ever speak again.

'Your asthma's worse than you're letting on, isn't it?' He tapped the discharge report. 'According to this anyway.'

'It *was* bad at Craiglockhart, sir. But I can honestly say it was worse there than it ever was in France.'

'Well,' Mitchell said. 'Results posted this afternoon.' He smiled briskly. 'You won't have long to wait.'

TWO

Crude copies of Tenniel's drawings from *Alice in Wonderland* decorated one end of Ward Seven, for in peacetime this had been a children's hospital. Alice, tiny enough to swim in a sea of her own tears; Alice, unfolding like a telescope till she was nine feet tall; Alice, grown so large her arm protruded from the window; and, most strikingly, Alice with the serpent's neck, undulating above the trees.

Behind Rivers, a creaking trolley passed from bed to bed: the patients' breakfast dishes were being cleared away.

'Come on, Captain McBride, drink up,' Sister Roberts said, crackling past. 'We've not got all day, you know.'

This was said loudly, for *his* benefit. He'd arrived on the ward too early, before they were ready for him.

'You knew him, didn't you?' Elliot Smith said, coming up to him, looking over his shoulder.

Rivers looked puzzled.

'Lewis Carroll.'

'Oh, yes. Yes.'

'What was he like?'

Rivers spread his hands.

'Did you like him?'

'I think I wanted him very much to like me. And he didn't.' A slight smile. 'I'm probably the last person to ask about him.'

Elliot Smith pointed to the snake-neck. 'That's interesting, isn't it?'

'Ready now, Captain Rivers,' Sister Roberts said. They watched her march off.

'"*Captain*,"' Elliot Smith murmured.

'I'm in the dog house,' Rivers said. 'I only get "Dr" when she approves of me.'

Behind the screens Ian Moffet lay naked from the waist down. He looked defiant, nervous, full of fragile, ungrounded pride. His skin had a greenish pallor, though that might merely be the reflection of light from the green screens that surrounded his bed, creating a world, a rock pool full of secret life. Rivers pushed one screen back so that light from the window flooded in. Now Moffet's legs, stretched out on the counterpane, were the dense grey-white of big, cheap cod. Muscles flabby but not wasted, as they would have been in a case of spinal injury, though he'd been unable to walk for more than three months, an unusually long time for hysterical paralysis to persist.

The history was, in one sense, simple. Moffet had fallen down in a 'fainting fit' while on his way to the Front, shortly after hearing the guns for the first time. When he recovered consciousness he could not move his legs.

'It was ridiculous to *expect* me to go to the Front,' he'd said in their first interview. 'I can't stand noise. I've never been able to stay in the same room as a champagne cork popping.'

You poor blighter, Rivers had thought, startled out of compassion. More than any other patient Moffet brought the words 'Pull yourself together, man' to the brink of his lips.

'Why didn't you apply for exemption?' he'd asked instead.

Moffet had looked at him as if he'd just been accused of eating peas from a knife. 'One is not a pacifist.'

He'd tried everything with Moffet. No, he hadn't. He'd not, for example, tried attaching electrodes to Moffet's legs and throwing the switch, as Dr Yealland would certainly have done by now. He'd not held tubes of radium against his skin till it burnt. He'd not given him subcutaneous injections of ether. All these things were being done to get men back to the Front or keep them there. He'd not even hypnotized him. What he'd actually tried was reason. He didn't *like* what he was going to do now, but it had become apparent that, until Moffet's reliance on the physical symptom was broken, no more rational approach stood any chance of working.

'You understand what I'm going to do?' he asked.

'I *know* what you're going to do.'

Rivers smiled. 'Tell me, then.'

'Well, as far as I can make out, you . . . er . . . intend to draw . . .' Minute muscles twitched round Moffet's nose and lips, giving him the look of a supercilious rabbit. '*Stocking tops?* On my legs, here.' With delicately pointed fingers he traced two lines across the tops of his thighs. 'And then, gradually, day by day, you propose to . . . um . . . *lower* the stockings, and as the stockings are *unrolled*, so to speak, the . . . er . . . paralysis will . . .' A positive orgy of twitching. 'Retreat.'

'That's right.'

Moffet's voice drooled contempt. 'And you have no doubt this procedure will work?'

Rivers looked into the pupils of his eyes so intently that for a moment he registered no colour except black. 'None whatsoever.'

Moffet stared at him, then turned away.

'Shall we get started?' Rivers lifted Moffet's left leg and began to draw a thick black line on to his skin, two inches below the fold of the groin.

'I hope that's not indelible.'

'Of course it's not. I'm going to have to wash it off in the morning.'

Rivers looked at the length of Moffet's legs and tried to calculate how long it was going to take him to reach the toes. Two weeks? And that would have to include Sundays, which put paid to his plans for a weekend in Ramsgate with his sisters. Katharine was far from well; in fact she was virtually bedridden and for much the same reasons as Moffet. Rivers frowned with concentration as he carried the pencil line under the thigh. Moffet's flabby skin kept snagging the pencil point.

Elliot Smith's comment on the serpent: 'That's interesting.' It was no more than he'd thought himself. Evidently snakes had lost the right to be simply snakes. Dodgson had hated them, a quite exceptionally intense hatred, and the woods round Knowles Bank were full of them, particularly in spring when you regularly stumbled across knots of adders, as many as thirty or forty sometimes, drowsy from their winter sleep. They'd gone for a walk once, the whole family, Ethel and Katharine holding Dodgson's hands, himself and Charles trailing behind, imitating his rather prissy, constipated-hen walk, though careful not to let their father catch them at it. They rounded a bend, Dodgson and the girls leading, and there, right in the centre of the path, was a snake. Zigzag markings, black on yellow, orange eyes, forked tongue flickering out of that wide, cynical (anthropomorphic rubbish) mouth. Dodgson went white. He sat down, collapsed rather, on a tree stump and the girls fanned him with their hats, while father caught the snake in a cleft stick and threw it far away, a black *s* against the sky unravelling as it fell.

Later he went back to look for it, spending an

hour searching through the flamy bracken, but only found a cast-off skin draped over a stone, transparent, the brilliant markings faded, the ghost of a snake.

Why was the devil shown in the form of a snake? he asked his father, because it was the only question he knew how to ask.

Later there'd been other questions, other ways of finding answers. Once, while he was home for the weekend, Katharine sat on an adder, and ran home screaming. He'd gone straight out and killed it, or so he thought, intending to dissect it at Bart's. Finding the family in the drawing-room, he'd tipped the snake out on to the hearthrug to show them, and found himself confronted by an adder that was very far from dead. The girls screamed and hid behind the sofa, while he and his father and Charles trampled it to death.

How do you think about an incident like that *now*? he wondered, beginning the second circle. Probably every generation thinks the world of its youth has been changed past recognition, but he thought for his generation – Moffet's too, of course – the task of making meaningful connections was quite unusually difficult. A good deal of innocence had been lost in recent years. Not all of it on battlefields.

He lowered Moffet's leg and walked round the bed. From here he could see, through a gap in the screens, the drawings of Alice. Suddenly, with Moffet's paralysed leg clamped to his side as he closed the circle, Rivers saw the drawings not as an irrelevance, left over from the days when this had been a children's ward, but as cruelly, savagely appropriate. All those bodily transformations causing all those problems. *But they solved them too.* Alice in Hysterialand.

'There,' he said, putting the leg down. 'Now can you prop yourself up a bit?'

Moffet raised himself on to his elbows and looked down at his legs. 'Quite apart from anything else,' he said, enunciating each word distinctly, 'it looks bloody obscene.'

Rivers looked down. 'Ye-es,' he agreed. 'But it won't when we get below the knee. And *tomorrow* the sensation in this area' – he measured it out with his forefingers – 'will be normal.'

Their eyes met. Moffet would have liked to deny it was possible, but his gaze shifted. He'd already begun to invest the circles with power.

Rivers touched his shoulder. 'See you tomorrow morning,' he said.

Quickly, he ran downstairs and plunged into the warren of corridors, wondering if he'd have time to read the files on the new patients before the first of them arrived for his appointment. He glanced at his watch, and something about the action tweaked his memory. Now that *would* be 'interesting', he thought. An innocent young boy becomes aware that he is the object of an adult's abnormal affection. Put bluntly, the Rev. Charles Do-do-do-

Dodgson can't keep his hands off him, *but* – thanks to that gentleman's formidable conscience – nothing untoward occurs. The years pass, puberty arrives, friendship fades. In the adult life of that child no abnormality appears, except perhaps for a certain difficulty in integrating the sexual drive with the rest of the personality (What do you mean 'perhaps'? he asked himself), until, in middle age, the patient begins to suffer from the delusion that he is turning into an extremely large, eccentrically dressed white rabbit, forever running down corridors consulting its watch. What a case history. Pity it didn't happen, he thought, pushing the door of his consulting-room open, it would account for quite a lot.

He thought, sometimes, he understood Katharine's childhood better than his own.

Cheshire Cat! Cheshire Cat! he and Charles had chanted as she sat enthroned in Dodgson's lap, grinning from ear to ear. The nickname, so casually bestowed, had lasted all her childhood, and his only consolation was she hadn't minded it a bit. Poor Kath, she'd had little enough to smile about since.

Files, he told himself. He took them out of his briefcase and started to read. Geoffrey Wansbeck, twenty-two years old. Wansbeck had – well, *murdered*, he supposed the word would have to be – a German prisoner, for no better reason (Wansbeck said) than that he was feeling tired and irritable and resented having to escort the man back from the line. For . . . eight months – in fact, nearer ten – he'd experienced no remorse, but then, while in hospital recovering from a minor wound, he'd started to suffer from hypnagogic hallucinations in which he would wake suddenly to find the dead German standing by his bed. Always, accompanying the visual hallucination, would be the reek of decomposition. After a few weeks the olfactory hallucination began to occur independently, only now the smell seemed to emanate from Wansbeck himself. He was convinced others could smell it and, no matter how often he was reassured, avoided close contact with other people as much as he could.

Hmm. Rivers took off his glasses and rubbed his eyes, swinging his chair round to face the window. He'd had a bad night and was finding it difficult to concentrate. Late August sunlight, the colour of cider, streamed into the room, and he was suddenly seized by sadness, a banal, calendar-dictated sadness, for the past summer and all the summers that were past.

At dinner one evening Mr Dodgson had leant across to mother and said, 'I l-l-l-love all ch-ch-ch-ch-'

'Train won't start,' Charles had whispered.

'Children, M-Mrs R-Rivers, as l-l-l-long as they're g-g-g-girls.'

He had looked down the table at the two boys, and it had seemed to Rivers that the sheer force of his animosity had loosened his tongue.

'Boys are a mistake.'

Charles hadn't minded that Mr Dodgson disliked

them, but *he* had. Mr Dodgson was the first adult he'd met who stammered as badly as he did himself, and the rejection hurt.

'Are w-we a m-m-m-m-mistake?' he'd asked his mother at bedtime. 'W-why are w-we?'

'Of course you're not a mistake,' his mother had said, smoothing the hair back from his forehead.

'So w-why d-d-does h-he s-say w-w-w-w-we are?'

'I expect he just likes girls more than boys.'

'B–b-b-b-but w-w-why d-d-does he?'

Wansbeck's eyes were inflamed, whether from crying or because of his cold was difficult to tell.

Rivers waited for the latest paroxysm of coughing to pass. 'You know we don't *have* to do this now. I can equally well see you when you're feeling better.'

Wansbeck wiped his raw nose on the back of his hand. 'No, I'd rather get it over with.' He shifted in his seat, flicking his tongue over cracked lips, and gazed fretfully round the room. 'Do you think we could have the window open?'

Rivers looked surprised – in spite of the sunshine, the wind was bitingly cold – but he got up and opened the window, realizing, as he did so, that Wansbeck's request was prompted by his fear of the smell. The breeze sucked the net curtains through the gap. Rivers went back to his chair and waited.

'I used a bayonet I found on a corpse. We were going through a wood, and there'd been a lot of heavy fighting. I remember the man I took it from, he'd died with an expression of absolute agony on his face. Big man, very dark, lot of blood round his nose, black, covered with flies, a sort of . . . buzzing moustache. I remember him better than the man I killed. He was walking ahead of me, I couldn't do it in his back, so I shouted at him to turn round. He knew straight away. I stuck it in, and he screamed, and . . . I pulled it out, and stuck it in. And again. And again. He was on the ground and it was easier. He kept saying, *"Bitte, Bitte,"* and putting his hands . . .' Wansbeck raised his own, palms outwards. 'The odd thing was I heard it in English. Bitter, bitter. I knew the word, but I didn't register what it meant.'

'Would it have made a difference?'

A puckering of the lips.

'What were you thinking about immediately before you picked up the bayonet?'

'Nothing.'

'Nothing at all?'

'I just wanted to go to sleep, and this bastard was stopping me.'

'How long had you been in the line?'

'Twelve days.' Wansbeck shook his head. 'Not good enough.'

'What isn't good enough?'

'That. As an excuse.'

'Reasons aren't excuses.'

'No?'

Rivers was thinking deeply. 'What do you think I can do to help?'

'Nothing. With respect.'

'Oh, damn that.'

Wansbeck smiled. 'As you say.' He held his handkerchief to his mouth as another fit of coughing seized him. 'I'll try not to give you this at least.'

Wansbeck was a man of exceptionally good physique, tall, broad-shouldered, deep-chested. Rivers, estimating height, weight, muscular tone, noting the tremor of the huge hands, a slight twitch of the left eyelid, was aware, at a different level, of the pathos of a strong body broken – though he didn't know why the word 'broken' should occur to him, since, objectively speaking, Wansbeck's physical suffering amounted to nothing more than a bad cold. He'd made a good recovery from his wound.

'When did you first notice the smell?'

'In the hospital. Look, everybody goes on about the smell. I *know* there isn't one.' A faint smile. 'It's just I can still smell it.'

'When was the first time?'

'I was in a side ward. Three beds. One man quite bad, he'd got a piece of shrapnel stuck in his back. He was called Jessop, not that it matters. The other was a slight arm wound, and he was obviously getting better and I realized there was a chance I'd be left alone with Jessop. The one who couldn't move. And I started to worry about it, because he was helpless and I knew if I wanted to kill him I could.'

'Did you dislike him at all? Jessop.'

'Not in the least. No.'

'So it was just the fact that he was helpless?'

Wansbeck thought a moment. 'Yes.'

'*Were* you left alone with him?'

'Yes.'

'What happened?'

A sound midway between a snort and a laugh. 'It was a long night.'

'Did you want to kill him?'

'Yes –'

'No, *think*. Did you *want* to kill him or were you *afraid* of wanting to kill him?'

Silence. 'I don't know. What difference does it make?'

'Enormous.'

'Afraid. I *think*. After that I asked if I could go on to the main ward. And to answer your question, the first time I noticed the smell was the following morning.' A long silence, during which he started to speak several times before eventually saying, 'You know when I told the doctor about not wanting to be left alone with Jessop, he said, "How long have you suffered from homosexual impulses?"' A quick, casual glance, but Wansbeck couldn't disguise his anger. 'I didn't want to to to *fuck* him, I wanted to *kill* him.'

'Does it still bother you to be alone with people?'

Wansbeck glanced round the room. 'I avoid it when I can.'

They exchanged smiles. Wansbeck put his hand up and stroked his neck.

'Is your throat bothering you?'

'Bit sore.'

Rivers went round the desk and felt his glands. Wansbeck stared past him with a strained look. Evidently the smell was particularly bad. 'Yes, they are a bit swollen.' He touched Wansbeck's forehead, then checked his pulse. 'I think you'd be better off in bed.'

Wansbeck nodded. 'You know, I can tell the smell isn't real, because I can still smell it. I'm too bunged up to smell anything else.'

Rivers smiled. He was starting to like Wansbeck. 'Tell Sister Roberts I've told you to go to bed, and would she take your temperature, please. I'll be up to see you later.'

At the door Wansbeck turned. 'Thank you for what you *didn't* say.'

'And what's that?'

'"It was only a boche – if it was up to me I'd give you a medal. Nobody's going to *hang* you for it."'

'You mean other people *have* said that?'

'Oh, yes. It never seems to occur to them that punishment might be a relief.'

Rivers looked hard at him. 'Self-administered?'

'No.'

A fractional hesitation?

'Go to bed,' Rivers said. 'I'll be up in a minute.'

After Wansbeck had gone, Rivers went to close the

window, and stood for a moment watching boys playing in the square. High sharp cries, like seagulls.

'Are w-we a m-m-m-m-mistake? W-why are w-we?'

'Of course you're not a mistake,' his mother had said, smoothing the hair back from his forehead.

'So w-why d-d-does h-he s-say w-w-w-w-we are?'

'I expect he just likes girls more than boys.'

'B–b-b-b-but w-w-why d-d-does he?'

Rivers smiled. I know, he thought, I know. Questions, questions.

'Boys are rough and noisy. And they fight.'

'B-b-but you h-h-have to to to f-f-f-ight, s-s-sometimes.'

Yes.

THREE

Prior dawdled along, scuffing the sleeve of his tunic along the sea-wall, looking out over the pale, level, filthy sands to where the waves turned. Silence was a relief after the jabber of tongues in the mess: who was going out with the next draft, who was up for promotion, who had been recommended for an MC. The eyes that slid to your chest and then to your left sleeve. The cards, the gossip, the triviality, the muck-raking, the rubbish – he'd be glad to be shot of it all.

He was going back to France. He'd spent the evening writing to people: Sarah, his mother, Charles Manning, Rivers. And the last letter had reminded him of Craiglockhart, so that now he drifted along, remembering the light flashing on Rivers's glasses, and the everlasting *pok-pok* from the tennis courts that somehow wove itself into the pattern of their speech and silence, as Rivers extracted his memories of France from him, one by one, like a dentist pulling teeth.

He wondered what Rivers would think of his going back. Not much.

The beach was dark below him. They were all gone, the munitions workers and their girls, the war profiteers with stubby fingers turning the pages of *John Bull*. German boats came in close sometimes. 'Not close enough,' Owen had said, as they'd waited for the draft list to go up on the wall. And he'd laughed, with that slightly alarmed look he sometimes had.

A friendly, lolling, dog-on-its-back sort of sea. You could swim in that and not feel cold. He started to wander along with no idea of where his feet were taking him or why. After a few minutes he rounded the headland and looked along the half-circle of South Bay at the opposite cliffs, surmounted by their white Georgian terraces. Some of his brother officers were up there now, living it up at the most expensive of the town's oyster bars. He'd been there himself two nights ago, but tonight he didn't fancy it.

Closer at hand were souvenir shops, coconut-shies, swing-boats, funny hats, the crack of rifle fire, screams of terror from the haunted house where cardboard skeletons leapt out of the cupboards with green electric light bulbs flashing in the sockets of their skulls. If they'd seen . . . *Oh, leave it, leave it.*

Behind him, along the road that led to the barracks, were prim boarding-houses with thick lace curtains that screened out the vulgarity of daytrippers. You couldn't go for a walk anywhere in

Scarborough without seeing the English class system laid out before you in all its full, intricate horror.

He heard a gasp of pain beside him, and a hand clutched his sleeve. A red-haired woman, flashily dressed and alone. 'Sorry, love, it's these shoes.' She smiled brightly at him. 'I keep going over on the heel.'

She rested her arms beside his on the railings, her right elbow lightly touching his sleeve.

'No, thanks.'

'Why, you been offered summat?'

She muttered on. It had come to summat if a decent woman couldn't have a rest without being . . . *pestered*. And who did he think he was anyway? Couple of bits of gold braid, they think their shit smells of violets –

'I don't pay.'

A whoop of laughter. 'Well, you're certainly not getting it free.'

He smiled, allowing a note of pathos to creep into his voice. 'I'm going back to France next week.'

'Aw, piss off.'

For a moment he hoped she might take her own advice, but she didn't. They stood side by side, almost touching, but he was miles away, remembering Lizzie MacDowell and the first day of the war. 'Long Liz' they called her, for, among the girls who worked Commercial Road, most of them reared in the workhouse, Lizzie's height – a full five feet no

less – made her a giant. She was his best friend's
mother, a fact not at the forefront of his mind when
he met her in a back alley on his way home from the
pub and told her he'd enlisted.

– *Good lad!* she'd said.

Lizzie was a great enthusiast for the Empire. And
somehow or other he'd gone home with her, stumbling up the passage and into the back bedroom,
until finally, in a film of cooling sweat, they'd lain
together on the sagging bed, while the bedbugs
feasted and a smell of urine rose from the chamberpot
underneath. She'd told him about her regulars. One
man came every month, turned a chair upside-down
and shoved each one of the four legs in turn up his
arse. Didn't want her to do anything, she said. Just
watch.

– *Well, you know what a worry-guts I am. I keep
thinking what'll I do if he gets stuck?*

– *Saw the bloody leg off.*

– *Do you mind, that's the only decent chair I've got.*

'What's so funny?'

'Just thinking about an old friend.'

Money had not changed hands on that occasion.
He'd been Lizzie's patriotic gesture: one of seven.
Poor Lizzie, she'd been very disillusioned when five
of the seven turned out not to have enlisted at all.

'Do you fancy a bit of company, then?'

He looked at her. 'You don't give up, do you?'
And then suddenly the shrieks, the rattle of rifle fire,
pub doors belching smells of warm beer were intoler-

able. Anything not to have to go on being the oil bead on this filthy water. 'All right.'

She was telling the truth about her shoes. If she hadn't clung to his arm she'd have fallen over more than once as they climbed the steep steps to the quieter streets behind the foreshore.

'What do they call you?' she asked, breathing port into his face.

'Billy. You?'

'Elinor.'

I'll bet, he thought. 'D' y' get "Nellie"?'

'Sometimes,' she said, her voice pinched with dignity. 'It's just round the corner here.' Perhaps she sensed he was having second thoughts for her arm tightened. ''S not far.'

They went up a flight of steps to the door. As she fumbled with the key he looked round, and almost stumbled over a cluster of unwashed milk bottles, furred green.

'*Mind,*' she said. 'You'll have everybody out.'

The hall dark, smelling of drains and mice. A face – no more than a slit of sallow skin and one eye – peered through a crack in the door on his left.

'You'll have to be quiet,' Nellie whispered, and then, catching sight of the face just as the door closed, yelled, 'There's some right nosy bastards round here.'

They walked up the stairs, arms round each other's waists, shoulders and hips bumping in the narrow space, catching the breath of each other's laughter, until her tipsiness communicated itself to him and all doubt and reluctance dissolved away.

She unlocked the door. A naked overhead bulb revealed a tousled bed, a chair piled high with camisoles and stays, a wash-stand and – surprisingly businesslike, this – a clean towel and a bar of yellow soap.

'You won't mind having a little wash.'

He didn't *mind*. He was buggered if he'd rely on it, though.

'Do you know,' she said, unbuttoning her blouse, 'I had one poor lad the other week washed his *hands*?'

Prior tugged at his tie, looking around for somewhere to put his clothes, and noticed a chair by the fireplace. Rather a grand fireplace, with a garland of flowers and fruit carved into the mantel, but boarded up now, of course, and a gas fire set into it. He was pulling his half-unbuttoned tunic over his head when he noticed a smell of gas. Faint but unmistakable. Tented in dark khaki, he fought back the rush of panic, sweat streaming down his sides, not the gradual sweat of exercise but a sudden drench, rank, slippery, hot, then immediately cold. He freed himself from the tunic and went to open the window, looking out over sharp-angled, moonlit roofs to the sea. He told himself there was no reason to be afraid, but he was afraid. All the usual reactions: dry mouth, wet armpits, skipping heart, the bulge in the throat that makes you cough. Tight scrotum, shrivelled cock.

Jesus Christ, he was going to have to put a johnny on that, talk about a kid in its father's overcoat. He heard his own voice, awkward, sounding younger than he felt. 'I'm afraid this isn't going to work.'

'Aw, don't say that, love, it'll be al –'

Phoney warmth. She was used to pumping up limp pricks.

'No, it won't.'

He came back into the room and looked at her. Her hair had fallen across her shoulders, not in a cloudy mass but in distinct coils, precise crescents, like you see on the floor of a barber's shop. He picked up one of the coils and wound it round his fingers. Red stripes marked the places where the bones of her stays bit into the skin. Catching the direction of his glance, she rubbed ineffectually at them. He wasn't behaving as clients generally behaved, and any departure from the usual run of things made her nervous. Two people's fear in the room now. But her gaze remained steady, surprisingly steady, when you thought that only five minutes ago she'd been too tipsy to walk straight. *Now* ... well, she'd had a few, but she certainly wasn't drunk. Perhaps she needed the mask of drunkenness more than she needed drink.

'Have I got a spot on the end of me conk or what?'

'No,' he said stupidly.

They stared at each other.

'Wouldn't hurt to lie down,' she said.

He finished undressing, reached out and tentatively took the weight of her breasts in his hands. So far, he realized, he hadn't had the shopping list, the awful litany that started whenever you met a woman's eyes in Covent Garden or the Strand. '. . . and five bob extra to suck me tits.'

'Two quid,' she said, reading his thoughts. 'On the table there.'

He got into bed, telling himself the cold damp patch under his left buttock was imagination. He put his hand down. It wasn't. Dotted here and there on the sheet were tiny coils of pubic hair. He wondered whose spunk he was lying in, whether he knew him, how carefully she'd washed afterwards. He groped around in his mind for the appropriate feeling of disgust, and found excitement instead, no, more than that, the sober certainty of power.

All the men who'd passed through, through Scarborough, through her, on their way to the Front . . . And how many of them dead? As she squatted over the bowl to wash – a token affair, he was glad to see – he felt them gathering in the hall, thronging the narrow stair, pressing against the door. Halted on the threshold only by the glare of light.

'Can we have that out?' he said. 'It's in my eyes.'

And now they were free to enter. Waiting, though, till the springs creaked and sagged beneath her weight. His hands were their hands, their famished eyes were his. Pupils strained wide in starlight fastened on a creamy belly and a smudge of dark hair.

He stroked and murmured and her fingers closed round him. 'There you are, you see. I told you it'd be all right.'

He fucked her slowly. After a while her hands came round and grasped his arse, nails digging in, though whether this was a pretence to hurry things along or a genuine flicker of response he couldn't tell. He was aware of their weight on him, his arms were braced to carry it . . .

And then something went wrong. He looked down at the shuttered face and recognized the look, recognized it not with his eyes but with the muscles of his own face, for he too had lain like this, waiting for it to be over. A full year of fucking, before he managed to come, on the narrow monastic bed, a crucifix above it, on the far wall – he would never forget it – a picture of St Lawrence roasting on his grid. The first time Father Mackenzie knelt, holding him round the waist, crying, *We really touched bottom that time, didn't we?* One way of putting it, but *we*? What the fuck did he mean by *we*? Later – though not much later, he'd been a forward child – he'd begun to charge, not so much resorting to prostitution as inventing it, for he knew of nobody else who got money that way. First Father Mackenzie. Then others.

The only way not to be her was to hate her. Narrowing his eyes, he blurred her features, ran them together into the face they pinned to the revolver targets. A snarling, baby-eating boche. But they didn't want that, the men who used his eyes and hands as theirs. He felt them withdraw, like a wave falling back.

All right, then, for *me*. He lowered his forehead on to hers, knowing without having to be told that she wouldn't let him kiss her. She wriggled beneath him, and he lifted his weight. Slowly and deliberately, she put her index finger deep into her mouth, and brought it out with a startling *pop*, and then – he had time to guess what she intended – scratched the small of his back delicately so that he shivered and thrust deeper, and rammed the finger hard up his arse. *Ah*, he cried, more with shock than pleasure, but already he was bursting, spilling, falling towards her, gasping for breath, laughing, gasping again, tears stinging his eyes as he rolled off her and lay still. Hoist on his own petard. That had always been one of *his* tricks to speed the unreasonably lingering guest.

She got up immediately and squatted over the bowl. He took the hint and started to dress, sniffing round the fireplace as he buttoned his tunic.

'What's the marra with *you*?'

'I thought I could smell gas.'

'Oh that, yeh, you probably can. Tap leaks. I'm tired of telling her.'

He wouldn't do this again, he decided, buckling his belt. It might work for some men, but . . . not for him. For him, it was all slip and slither, running across shingle. He hadn't been sure at the end who was fucking who. Even the excitement he'd felt at the idea of sliding in on another man's spunk was ambiguous, to say the least. Not that he minded ambiguity – he couldn't have lived at all if he'd minded *that* – but this was the kind of ambiguity people hide behind. And he was too proud to hide.

On his way back to the barracks he forgot her. A few hundred yards from the gate he drew level with a group of officers. Most had paced themselves well, and were now rather more sober than they'd been when he bumped into them earlier in the evening. But Dalrymple was in a desperate state, striding along with the exalted, visionary look of somebody whose sole aim in life is to get to the lavatory in time.

'Will he be all right?' Prior asked.

'We'll get him there,' said Bainbrigge.

As they entered the barracks gates, thunder rumbled on the horizon; the clouds were briefly lit by lightning. Prior waited till the crowd cleared before going across to the main building to get washed, thinking, as he stripped off and splashed cold water over his chest and groin, that a deserted wash-room at night, all white tiles and naked lights, is the most convincing portrayal of hell the human mind can devise. He peered into the brown-spotted glass, remembering the moment when Nellie's face had dissolved into the face of the boche target.

– *What's the worst thing you could have done?* Rivers asked.

A phoney question. Rivers didn't believe in the worst things. He thought Prior was being histrionic. And perhaps I was, Prior thought, staring into the glass at the row of empty cubicles behind him, feeling 'the worst things' crowd in behind him, jostling for the privilege of breathing down his neck. He'd even, coming to himself at four or five o'clock in the morning with no idea of how the night had been spent, thought it possible he might have killed somebody. And yet, why should that be 'the worst thing'? His reflection stared back at him, hollow-eyed. Murder was only killing in the wrong place.

The wind was rising as he hurried across the gritty tarmac to his tent. Bent double, he braced himself to face the smell of armpits and socks, heavy on the day's stored heat, for though they left the flaps open, nothing could prevent the tents becoming ovens in hot weather. He took a deep breath, as deep as he could manage, and crawled into the stinking dark.

A voice said, 'Hello.'

Of course. Hallet. The past week he'd had the tent to himself, because Hallet had been away on a bombing course in Ripon.

'Can you see all right?'

The beam of a torch illuminated yellow grass littered with cigarette butts.

'I can manage, thanks.'

Blinking to reaccustom himself to the blackness, Prior wriggled into his sleeping-bag.

'You're just back from London, aren't you?'

He resigned himself to having to talk. 'Yes. Week ago.'

A flicker of lightning found the whites of Hallet's eyes. 'Have you been boarded yet?'

'Out next draft. You?'

'Next draft.'

Voice casual, but the mouth dry.

'First time?' Prior asked.

'Yes, as a matter of fact it is.'

Now that Prior was accustomed to the gloom he could see Hallet clearly: olive-skinned, almost Mediterranean-looking, a nice crooked mouth with prominent front teeth that he was evidently self-conscious about, for he kept pulling his upper lip down to hide them. Quite fetching. Not that in these circumstances Prior ever permitted himself to be fetched.

'I'm really rather looking forward to it.'

The words hung on the air, obviously requiring an answer of some kind, but then what could one say? He was scared shitless, he was *right* to be scared shitless, and any 'reassuring' remark risked drawing attention to one or other of these unfortunate facts.

'Some of the men in my platoon have been out three times,' Hallet said. 'I think that's the only thing that bothers me, really. How the hell do you lead men who know more than you do?'

'You pray for a good sergeant. A really good sergeant tells you what orders to give him, doesn't let anybody else see him doing it, and doesn't let himself know he's doing it.'

'How many times have you – ?'

'This'll be the fourth. Wound, shell-shock, trench fever. Not in that order.'

Hallet was lying on his back, hands clasped behind his head, nothing much visible from Prior's angle except his chin. How appallingly random it all was. If Hallet's father had got a gleam in his eye two years later than he did, Hallet wouldn't be here. He might even have missed the war altogether, perhaps spent the rest of his life goaded by the irrational shame of having escaped. 'Cowed subjection to the ghosts of friends who died.' That was it exactly, couldn't be better put. Ghosts everywhere. Even the living were only ghosts in the making. You learned to ration your commitment to them. This moment in this tent already had the quality of *remembered* experience. Or perhaps he was simply getting old. But then, after all, in trench time he *was* old. A generation lasted six months, less than that on the Somme, barely twelve weeks. He was this boy's great-grandfather.

He looked at Hallet again, at the warm column of his neck, and tried to think of something to say, something light-hearted and easy, but could think of nothing. He stared instead at the stained canvas, lit by flickers of summer lightning, and noticed that the largest stain looked like a map of Africa.

FOUR

Two black lines circled Moffet's legs immediately above the knee.

'Close your eyes,' Rivers said. 'I want you to tell me exactly what you feel.'

'Pinprick.'

'How many?'

The pins touched again.

'Two.'

Again.

'One.'

Again.

'Two.' Moffett sounded bored. 'Two. Two.' A pause. 'Not sure.'

'All right. You can open your eyes now.'

He hadn't lied once. He'd lain with closed eyes, a fluttering visible beneath the thin lids, and Rivers had read in every line and fold of his face the temptation to lie, and yet the progression of yeses and noes had been totally accurate. True, he couldn't have hoped to lie convincingly, or not for long, but it was interesting that he hadn't tried. This was pure hysteria, uncontaminated by malingering.

'Rivers, do you ever think you were born into the wrong century?'

Rivers looked surprised. 'Survived into, perhaps.'

'It's just this reminds me of seventeenth-century witch-finders, you know? They used to stick pins in people too.'

'I expect they were looking for the same thing. Areas of abnormal sensation.'

'Do you think they found them?'

Rivers lifted Moffet's left leg and began to draw a line three inches lower than the line he'd drawn yesterday morning. 'I don't see why not. Some witches were probably hysterics. At least a lot of the reported phenomena suggest that.'

'And the witch-*finders*?'

'I don't know. Simpler. Nastier.'

'I don't like that word. Applied to this.'

'Hysteria?' He could quite see that 'shell-shock', useless and inaccurate though the term was, might appeal to Moffet rather more. It did at least sound appropriately male. 'I don't think anybody likes it. The trouble is nobody likes the alternatives either.'

'It derives,' Moffet continued, hardening his voice, 'from the Greek *hysterā*. The womb.'

'Yes,' Rivers said dryly. 'I know.'

The problem with Moffet was that he was too intelligent to be satisfied with such a crude solution as paralysis. Hysterical symptoms of this gross kind — paralysis, deafness, blindness, muteness — occurred quite frequently in the immediate aftermath of trauma but they normally lingered only in those who were either uneducated or frankly stupid. Moffet was neither.

And whether this rather dramatic form of treatment was helping . . . Oh, it would get rid of the paralysis, but was there not the possibility that it might also reinforce a belief in magical solutions? Rivers sighed and walked round the bed. All his instincts were against it, but he knew it would get Moffet on his feet again. A witch-doctor could do this, he thought, beginning to draw, and probably better than I can. Come to think of it, there was *one* person who'd have done it brilliantly . . .

In Melanesia he'd quickly formed the habit of accompanying Njiru on his rounds. They would set off together, always in single file, because the path winding through thick bush was too narrow for them to walk abreast.

Seen from the rear, the extent of Njiru's spinal curvature was dreadfully apparent. Rivers wondered how such deformities were explained — which spirit inflicted them, and why? Sweat stung his bitten eyelids — he kept having to wipe his forearm across his face. Mainly the heat, but partly also anxiety. It was a bit like your first day at a new school, he thought, knowing you've *got* to get things right and that your chances of getting them right are infinitesimal because you know *nothing*. Only at school, provided you start at the same time as everybody else, you can solve the problem by fading into the group, darting about with all the other little grey minnows, safety in the shoal, but here he was alone, except for Hocart, and Hocart had been running a fever ever since they arrived, and today had chosen to stay behind in their tent.

At the village he crawled into a hut and squatted on the earth floor, watching and listening, while Njiru attended to his patient. An old woman, evidently a regular to judge by the way she and Njiru laughed and joked together. She was introduced as Namboko Taru, though 'Namboko', which he at first took to be a name, turned out to be a title: 'widow'. The same word also meant 'widower', but was not used as a title when applied to men. Two more disconnected facts to add to his discouragingly small heap.

Namboko Taru lay down, pushing the strip of brown bark cloth she wore down far enough to expose her belly. Njiru poured coconut oil on to her abdomen and began a massage, while Rivers tried to find out what was wrong. Constipation, it appeared. Was it, he wanted to ask, in view of her age, chronic constipation, or had there been a recent change in bowel habit? And was it simply constipation, or was there alternating diarrhoea? But his attempts to convey 'alternating diarrhoea' in a mixture of pidgin and mime threatened to bring the proceedings to a halt entirely, and he gave up, while Namboko Taru wiped tears of laughter from her cheeks. He might not be contributing to the cure but he was certainly taking her mind off the condition.

Meanwhile the movements of Njiru's hands began to focus on a region below and to the left of the navel. He was chanting under his breath, swaying backwards and forwards, scooping the slack flesh together between the heel of his palms, like a woman gathering dough. The constant low murmur and the rhythmic movement were hypnotic. Suddenly, with a barking cry, Njiru seemed to catch something, shielded it in his cupped hands while he crawled to the door, and then threw it as far as he could into the bush. A brief conversation between doctor and patient, then Namboko Taru fastened her cloth and went into the bush, from whence, ten minutes later, a far happier woman emerged.

Meanwhile Rivers and Njiru talked. Namboko Taru's complaint belonged to a group of illnesses called *tagosoro*, which were inflicted by the spirit called Mateana. This particular condition − *nggasin* − was caused by an octopus that had taken up residence in the lower intestine, from where its tentacles might spread until they reached the throat. At this point the disease would prove fatal. As so often happened, one could detect behind the native belief the shadowy outline of a disease only too familiar to western medicine, though perhaps this was not a helpful way of looking at it. Namboko Taru believed she was cured. And certainly as a treatment for simple constipation the massage could hardly have been bettered, and had not differed in any essential respect from western massage, until very near the end.

Rivers pointed to himself and then to the coconut oil. Njiru nodded, poured oil into his palms and began the massage, chanting, rocking . . . Once again that curious hypnotic effect, a sense of being totally focused on, totally cared for. Njiru was a good doctor, however many octopi he located in the colon. The fingers probed deeper, the chanting quickened, the movements of the hands neared a climax, and then – nothing. Njiru sat back, smiling, terminating the physical contact as tactfully as he'd initiated it.

Rivers sketched the movement Njiru hadn't made. 'You no throw . . . *nggasin?*'

A gleam of irony. 'You no got *nggasin.*'

But *you* have, Rivers thought, sponging yesterday's black lines off Moffet's legs.

'And tomorrow,' he said authoritatively, measuring with his forefingers, 'this area will be normal.'

Moffet glared at him. 'You are consciously and deliberately destroying my self-respect.'

'I think you'll find that starts to come back once you're on your feet.'

Sister Carmichael was hovering on the other side of the screens, waiting to snatch the trolley from him. She was shocked by his insistence on doing everything himself, including the washing off of the previous lines. Consultants do not wash patients. *Nurses* wash patients. She would have been only marginally more distressed if she'd come on to the ward and found him mopping the floor. What he could not get across to her was that the rules of medicine are one thing, the rules of ritual drama quite another.

Wansbeck had had a bad night, she said, once the trolley had been snatched away. Temperature of 103, and he kept trying to open the window.

'All right, I'll see him next.'

The nurses had just finished sponging Wansbeck down, and he lay half naked, his skin a curdled bluish white against the snowy white of the sheets. As Rivers watched a shiver ran along his arms and chest, roughening and darkening the skin. They finished drying him, covered him up, and he was free to talk, though too weak to manage more than a few words.

Rivers was beginning to feel concerned about Wansbeck. Spanish influenza was quite unusually virulent and he had it badly, and yet he seemed indifferent to the outcome. Rivers grasped him firmly round the wrist. 'You know you've got to fight this.'

Probably 'fight' was the only word he understood. 'Done enough of that,' he muttered, and turned away.

In Westminster the leaves were already beginning to turn. Not to the brilliant reds and golds of the countryside, but a shabby tarnished yellow. In another few weeks they would start to fall. The worst thing about London was that summer ended so soon.

'You know, sometimes,' Rivers said carefully, his glasses flashing as he turned back from the window, 'it helps just to go back and try to to to to . . . gather things together. So. Let's see if I've got this right. You were in hospital after a riding accident –'

'Yes, that's right. I didn't notice the mare –'

'*Yes.* And while you were there, one of the nurses cut your penis off and put it in a jar of formaldehyde in the basement.'

Telford shook his head. 'I didn't say for for . . .'

'Formaldehyde. No, I know you didn't. They don't use pickling vinegar.'

'Ah, well, you see, you'd know that.'

A deep breath. 'Why do you think she did that?'

Telford shrugged. 'Dunno.'

'But you must have *wondered*. I mean it was quite an astonishing thing to do, wasn't it?'

'Wasn't for me to ask questions.' Telford leant forward, delivering what he obviously thought was the *coup de grâce*. 'You wouldn't want me teaching you *your* job, would you?'

At the moment he'd have welcomed assistance from any quarter. 'Didn't the doctor say anything?'

'Not a dicky bird.'

'Telford.' Rivers clasped his hands. 'What do you pee out of?'

'M'cock, you stupid bugger, what do you pee out of?'

Rivers concentrated on straightening his blotter. 'I wonder if it would help if we talked a little about women?'

It might have done. He was never to know. A few minutes later Telford said, 'I can't say I care for the tone of this conversation, Rivers. It may have escaped your notice, but we're not in a barracks.' He stood up. 'God knows, the last thing I want to do is pull rank, but I'd be grateful if you'd address me as *Major Telford* in future.'

He went out, slamming the door.

Moffet lay back, eyes closed, grinding, '*Yes, yes, yes, yes,*' as the pin pricked his skin.

The usual routine, and yet something was different. The air of indifference had gone. Deliberately, Rivers let the pin stray across the line on to skin that should still have been numb.

'*Yes, yes, yes.*'

The pin stopped. Moffet opened his eyes and smiled wearily. 'You can go all the way down if you like.' He closed his eyes again. Rivers moved the pin down the leg at intervals of two inches. 'Yes. Yes. Yes. Yes.' Wearily now, each 'yes' coming precisely at the moment the pin touched the skin. Over the shin, across the arch of the foot, down to the tip of the big toe. 'YES.'

Moffet had yelled the word. Through the gap in

the screens, Rivers saw the other patients turn and stare at the shrouded bed. He put the pin down. 'Well.'

He wasn't particularly surprised: the removal of hysterical paralysis was often – one might almost say generally – as dramatic as the onset. Moffet lay still, his face sallow against the whiteness of the pillow, making no attempt to hide his depression, and indeed why should he? His sole defence against the unbearable had been taken away and nothing put in its place.

'When did this happen?'

'First thing.'

'Have you tried to walk?'

'Not yet.'

'Do you want to?'

'Seems the logical next step. So to speak.'

'Can you swing yourself round? Sit on the side.'

Rivers knelt and began massaging Moffet's calves, chafing the slack flesh between his hands.

'I suppose I'm expected to be grateful.'

'No.' He stood up. 'All right, shall we try? Put your hands on my shoulders.'

Moffet levered himself off the edge of the bed.

'How does it feel?'

'Don't know. Weird.'

'Do you want to try a few steps?' Awkwardly, like untalented dancers, they shuffled across the floor, the curtains ballooning out around them. Rivers put his hands up and loosened Moffet's grip. 'No, you're all right, I've got you.' Two steps, then Moffet fell forward into his arms. Rivers lowered him back on to the bed. 'I think that's probably enough for now.'

Moffet collapsed against the pillows.

'It's important to keep at it, but I wouldn't try it just yet without an orderly.' He hesitated. 'You know we're going to have to talk about *why* this happened.'

He waited, but Moffet remained stubbornly silent.

'I'll be along again later.'

Later that afternoon, Major Telford – as he must now remember to call him – sidled up and tapped him discreetly on the shoulder. 'Yes, Major Telford, what is it?'

A conspiratorial whisper. 'Spot of bother in the latrines.'

Rivers followed him into the wash-room, wondering which bit of Telford's anatomy had dropped off now.

Telford pointed to the bathroom. 'Chap's been in there ages.'

'Yes, but –'

'Keeps groaning. Well, he did – stopped now.'

Rivers rattled the handle. 'Hello?'

'Tried that, it's locked.'

It couldn't be – there weren't any locks. Rivers lay down and looked under the door. A lot of water had slopped on to the floor, he could see an arm drooping over the edge of the bath – a puffy, white arm with blood oozing from the wrist. A chair had been wedged under the door handle. He tried pushing it, but it was no use. He stood up and kicked. The door was hardly thicker than cardboard – the bathrooms were mere cubicles put in cheaply when the War Office adapted the hospital for military use – and the second kick broke the hinges. He burst into the room, startled by his own face in the looking-glass. Moffet lay in the bath, pink water lapping the shining belly as it rose and fell. Breathing anyway. His head had slipped to one side, but his nostrils were clear of the water. A whisky bottle skittered across the floor as Rivers knelt by the bath. Cuts on both wrists, superficial on the right – deep on the left. Loss of blood probably fairly heavy, but you can never bloody well tell in water. He pushed Moffet's eyelids up, smelled his breath, felt for the pulse . . .

'Dead, is he?' Telford asked cheerfully.

Dead drunk. 'I think he'll be all right.'

Lack of space was the problem. Barely enough room to squeeze between the wash-basin and the bath at knee height. He had to bend from the waist to get his hands round Moffet's chest and then his fingertips slipped on the cold, plump skin. Telford stood, looking on.

'Get his legs.'

They heaved, but without co-ordination, Rivers finally managing to haul the shoulders out of the water just as Telford grew tired of waiting and dropped the legs back in. They were gasping for breath, shoulders bumping in the confined space.

'All right, together,' Rivers said. 'One, two . . .'

Moffet came clear, only to fall back with a splash, a great plume of water flying up and drenching them both.

'I'll try to get m'leg under him,' Telford said.

They lifted again, and Telford stepped into the water so that Moffet was balanced across his thigh, Rivers supporting the head and shoulders. They froze like that, an improbable and vaguely obscene *pietà*. 'All right?' Rivers asked.

'Right, I've got him.'

They collapsed in a heap on the floor, blood from Moffet's left wrist flowing more copiously now, bright, distinct drops splashing on to the mottled tiles. Rivers dragged a clean towel off the rail and pressed it hard against the deepest cut. 'There, you take over,' he said. 'I'll get Sister Roberts. Just press now, no need for anything else. *No tourniquets.*'

'Shouldn't dream of it,' Telford said, fluffing his shoulders.

Rivers intercepted Sister Roberts on her way down the ward. 'Moffet,' he said, pointing behind him. 'He's slashed his wrists. We need a wheelchair.'

He returned to find Telford entertaining the now semi-conscious Moffet with a story about an inexperienced groom who'd applied a tourniquet to the leg of his favourite hunter. 'Gangrene set in, would you believe? We had to shoot the poor sod.' Telford looked down at the fluttering lids. 'And it was only a graze.'

Moffet flapped like a landed fish, moaned, vomited yellow bile. Rivers tapped his cheek. 'Have you taken anything?'

Sister Roberts came creaking to the door with a wheelchair. Telford looked up at her, horrified, whipped a flannel off the side of the bath and draped it over Moffet's genitals.

'For God's sake, man,' Rivers snapped. 'She's a *nurse*.' Though with Telford's history it probably wasn't Sister Roberts's modesty he thought he was protecting. 'If you could get us a couple of blankets,' he said, twisting in the narrow space.

Moffet's head lolled to one side as they hauled him into the chair and wrapped blankets round him, though Rivers was beginning to suspect he was less drowsy than he seemed.

'Well,' he said, straightening up. 'I think I can manage now, Major Telford. Thank you, you've been a great help.'

'That's all right.' He looked down at Moffet and sniffed. 'Helps break up the afternoon. Anyway, what's all this Major nonsense?' he demanded, punching Rivers playfully in the biceps. 'Don't be such a stuffed shirt, man.'

And off he went, whistling 'A Bachelor Gay Am I'.

They wheeled Moffet into a side ward, since nothing is worse for morale on a 'shell-shock' ward than a suicide attempt. Except a successful suicide of course. He remembered the man at Craiglockhart who'd succeeded in hanging himself. Quite apart from his own tragedy he'd undone weeks of careful work on other people.

The deepest gash required stitching. Rivers set to work immediately, and was rather surprised to find Moffet stoical. He watched the needle dip in and out, only licking his lips once towards the end.

'There,' Rivers said. 'All done.'

Moffet rolled his head restlessly. 'I didn't make a very good job of it, did I?'

'Not many people do. The only person I've ever known to succeed by that method was a surgeon – he virtually severed his left hand.' He got up and stretched his legs, pressing a hand hard into the small of his back. 'How much whisky did you have?'

'Half a bottle. Bit more perhaps.'

No point talking to him, then.

'Where did you get it?'

'My mother. Does it matter?'

'And the razor?'

Moffet looked puzzled. 'Mine.'

'All right. You try to get some sleep.'

'Will you have to tell the police?'

'No.' Rivers looked down at him. 'You're a soldier. You're under military discipline.'

He found Sister Roberts waiting for him. 'I'm afraid we can't let this go,' he said. 'The lockers are supposed to be searched regularly.'

'I'll ask Miss Banbury. She was the last person to do it.'

She was also Sister Roberts's *bête noire*, for no better reason than that she was well-meaning, clumsy, enthusiastic, unqualified and upper class.

'His mother gave him the whisky.'

'Can't say I'm surprised. Silly woman.'

Sister Roberts, as he knew from numerous air-raid conversations of the previous winter, was the eldest girl in a family of eleven. She'd clawed her way out of the Gateshead slums and therefore felt obliged to believe in the corrosive effects on the human psyche of good food, good housing and good education.

'Telford was a bit of a revelation, wasn't he?' she said. 'Surprisingly cool.'

'Oh, Telford's fine. Until he opened his big mouth nobody noticed he was mad.' He added, not entirely as an afterthought, 'He works at the War Office.'

Outside in the corridor he met Wansbeck, now much better though surely not well enough to be up and about.

'How do you feel?' Rivers asked.

'Bit weak. Throat's still sore, but I'm not coughing as much.'

'You'd be better off in bed. Go on, back with you.'

As the doors banged shut behind Wansbeck, Rivers became aware of an insistent clicking. Nothing to account for it. The long corridor stretched ahead, empty, its grey, palely shining floor faintly marked with the shadows of the window frames. Click, click, click. And then he realized the sound was being caused by the bobbles on the end of the blind strings, tapping against each other in the slight breeze. But identifying the sound didn't seem to lessen its potency. It was almost the sound of a yacht's rigging, but the memory went deeper than that.

He had reached the lift before he managed to dredge it up. That day Njiru took him to see the skull houses at Pa Na Gundu, they'd walked for miles in sweltering heat, scarcely a breath of wind, and no sound except the buzzing of flies. Then, abruptly, they came out into a clearing, sharp blades of sunlight slanting down between the trees, and ahead of them, rising up the slope, six or seven skull houses, their gratings ornamented with strings of dangling shells. The feeling of being watched that skulls always gave you. Dazzled by the sudden light, he followed Njiru up the slope, towards a knot of shadows, and then one of the shadows moved, resolving itself into the shape of Nareti, the blind mortuary priest who squatted there, all pointed knees and elbows, snail trails of pus running from the corners of his eyes.

The furthest of the skull houses was being repaired, and its occupants had been taken out and arranged on the ground so that at first sight the clearing seemed to be cobbled with skulls. He'd hung back, not sure how close he was permitted to approach, and at that moment a sudden fierce gust of wind shook the trees and all the strings of votary shells rattled and clicked together.

The lift doors clanged open in his face, startling him back into the present day.

FIVE

Ada Lumb always wore black, less in mourning for her husband – if she'd ever had one – than because black enabled an air of awesome respectability to be maintained at minimal cost.

Respectability was Ada's god. She'd arrived in this neighbourhood eighteen years before, recently widowed, or so she claimed, with two pretty, immaculately dressed little girls in tow. The house had belonged to a man called Dirty Dick, who rambled and muttered and frightened children on street corners. Yellowing newspapers were stacked high in every room. Within a few weeks Ada had the house painted, doorstep scrubbed, range black-leaded, net curtains up at every window. At a safe distance from the house, she bought a lock-up shop, selling boiled boots, second-hand clothes and – below the counter – a great variety of patent medicines designed to procure abortion or cure clap. Pennyroyal Syrup, Dr Lawson's Cure for Female Blockages and

Obstructions, Dr Morse's Invigorating Cordial, Curtis's Manhood, Sir Samuel Hannay's Specific, Bumstead's Gleet Cure, The Unfortunate's Friend, and Davy's Lac-Elephantis, a foul-smelling suspension of chalk and God knows what, which claimed to be the medicated milk of elephants.

But on Sundays she locked up the shop and entertained the Vicar, the Rev. Arthur Lindsey, in a room which might have been designed as a stage set for the purpose. Dark oak furniture, plants with thick, durable, rubbery leaves – Ada had no patience with flowers, always drooping and dying – and, prominently displayed on a side table, the family Bible, open at a particularly fortifying text. In this setting Ada poured tea into china cups, dabbed her rat trap of a mouth with a starched napkin and engaged in light, or, in deference to the Sabbath, improving conversation on the topics of the day.

Billy Prior sat at the other end of the table, a concession to his new status as future son-in-law. No more material concessions had been forthcoming: he and Sarah had not been left alone together for a second. Though Ada was gratified by the engagement. She believed in marriage, the more strongly, Prior suspected, for never having sampled it herself. *You don't know that*, he reminded himself. But then he looked round the room and thought, *Yes, I do.* Photographs of Sarah and Cynthia stood on the sideboard, but none of the grandparents, none of their father. No portrait of Ada-the-blushing-bride.

And the fortifying text she'd selected for display was the chapter of the Book of Job in which Eliphaz the Temanite visits his friend and seeks to console him for the plague of boils which covers his skin from crown to sole by pointing out that he had it coming. One thing Ada *did* have was a sense of humour. Oh, and an eye for male flesh. Yesterday he'd helped her hang curtains, and her gaze on his groin as she handed the curtains up had been so frankly appraising he'd almost blushed. *You might fool Lindsey*, he thought, *but you don't fool me.*

He made an effort to attend to the conversation. They were talking about the granting of the vote to women of thirty and over, an act of which Ada strongly disapproved. It had pleased Almighty God, she said, to create the one sex visibly and unmistakably superior to the other, and that was all there was to be said in the matter. From the way Lindsey simpered and giggled, one could only assume he thought he knew which sex was meant. He was one of those Anglo-Catholic young men who waft about in a positive miasma of stale incense and seminal fluid. Prior knew the type – biblically as well.

Sarah touched the teapot, and stood up. 'I think this could do with freshening. Billy?'

'Does it take two of you, Sarah?'

'I need Billy to open the door, Mother.'

In the kitchen she burst out, 'Honestly, what century does she think she's living in?'

Prior shrugged. From the kitchen window

Melbourne Terrace sloped steeply down, a shoal of red-grey roofs half hidden in swathes of mist and rain. He wondered whether Ada had taken this house for the view, for the sweep of cobbled road, the rows and rows of smoking chimney-stacks, was as dramatic in its way as a mountain range, and, for Ada, rather more significant. For there, below her, was the life she'd saved her daughters from: scabby-mouthed children, women with black eyes, bedbugs, street fights, marriage lines pasted to the inside of the front window to humiliate neighbours who had none of their own to display. He could quite see how the vote might seem irrelevant to a woman engaged in such a battle.

Sarah came across and joined him by the window, putting her arms round his chest from behind and resting her face against his shoulder. 'I hope it's nicer tomorrow. You haven't had much luck with the weather, have you?'

Wasn't all he hadn't had. He turned to face her. 'When are we going to get some time alone?'

'I don't know.' She shook her head. 'I'll work something out.'

'Look, you could pretend to go to work, and —'

'I can't *pretend* to go to work, Billy. We need the money. Come on, she'll be wondering where we are.'

Prior found a plate of lardy cake thrust into his hand, and followed her back into the front room.

They found Lindsey confiding his ideas for next

week's sermon – he was attracted to the idea of sacrifice, he said. Are you indeed? thought Prior, plonking the plate down. Cynthia, not long widowed, was hanging on every word, probably on her mother's instructions: she was by far the more biddable of the two girls. Sitting down, Prior nudged Lindsey's foot under the table and was delighted to see a faint blush begin around the dog collar and work its way upwards. A sidelong, flickering glance, a brushing and shying away of eyes, and ... *You're wasting your lardy cake on that one, Ma,* Prior told his future mother-in-law silently, folding his arms.

After Lindsey had gone, Ada changed into her weekday dress and settled down with a bag of humbugs and a novel. She sat close to the fire, raising her skirt high enough to reveal elastic garters and an expanse of white thigh. As her skirt warmed through, a faint scent of urine rose from it, for Ada, as he knew from Sarah, followed the old custom and when taken short in the street straddled her legs like a mare and pissed in the gutter. His being allowed to witness these intimacies was another concession to the ring on Sarah's finger.

The young people gathered round the piano, and, after the requisite number of hymns had been thumped and bellowed through, passed on to sentimental favourites from before the war.

'You'll know this one, Ma,' Prior said, drawing

out the vowel sounds, ogling her over his shoulder. Rather to his surprise, she sang with him.

> For her beauty was sold,
> For an old man's gold,
> She's just a bird in a gilded cage!

'By heck, it was never my luck,' Ada said, going back to her book.

Prior glanced at his watch. 'Do you fancy a turn round the block?' he asked Sarah, closing the piano lid.

'Yes.' A quick glance at Cynthia.

'I'm too tired,' said Cynthia.

'You're never thinking of walking in this?' Ada said. 'Listen at it. It's blowing a gale.'

It was too.

'Anyway it's work tomorrow, our Sarah,' Ada said, closing her book. 'I think we'd all be better for an early night. Are you comfortable on that sofa, Billy?'

'Fine, thank you.' Except there's this ruddy great pole sticking into the cushions.

'You might try lying on your back.'

They'd have burnt her in the Middle Ages. Sarah brought down blankets and pillows from her bedroom, and, watched by Ada from the foot of the stairs, kissed him chastely goodnight.

It's my embarkation leave, he wanted to howl. We're engaged.

The door closed behind her. He wasn't ready for

bed – or rather he wasn't ready for bed *alone*. He took off his tunic and boots, wandered round the room, looked at photographs, finally threw himself on to the sofa and picked up Ada's discarded novel.

Ada had a great stock of books. A few romances, which she read with every appearance of enjoyment, gurgles of laughter erupting from the black bombazine like a hot spring from volcanic earth. But she preferred penny dreadfuls, which she read propped up against the milk bottle as she prepared the evening meal. Fingerprints, translucent with butter, encrusted with batter, sticky with jam, edged every page. Bloody thumbprints led up to one particularly gory murder. All the books had murders in them, all carried out by women. Aristocratic ladies ranged abroad, pushing their husbands into rivers, off balconies, over cliffs, under trains or, in the case of the more domestically inclined, feminine type of woman, remained at home and jalloped them to death. Only the final pages were free of cooking stains, and for a long time this puzzled him, until he realized that, in the final chapter, the adulterous murderesses were caught and punished. Ada had no truck with that. *Her* heroines got away with it.

The clock ticked loudly, as it had done all last night, a malevolent tick that kept him awake. He picked it up, intending to put it in the kitchen, but it stopped at once and only resumed its ticking when he replaced it on the mantel shelf. For Christ's sake, he thought, even the bloody clock's trained to keep its knees together.

He could hear the girls getting undressed in the room overhead: the thump of shoes being kicked off, snatches of conversation, giggles, almost – he convinced himself – the sigh of petticoats dropping to the floor. Sarah's momentary nakedness, before the white shroud of night-dress came down. He got up and went to the piano, stroking the keys, singing under his breath.

> Far, far from Wipers
> I long to be,
> Where German snipers
> Can't get at me.
>
> Damp is my dug-out,
> Cold are my feet
> Waiting for Whizzbangs
> To put me to sleep.

The door opened. He turned and saw Sarah, a white column of night-gown, a thick plait hanging down over her left shoulder.

'I'm sorry,' he said, closing the piano. 'Have I been making too much noise?'

'No, I just wanted to see you.'

Incredibly, impossibly, the sound of girlish whispering and giggling continued overhead.

'Cynthia,' Sarah said, closing the door. 'She's pretending I'm still there.'

She knelt on the hearthrug, and began feeding the few remaining sticks of wood into the fire. Then, carefully, so as not to douse the flames, she dropped shiny nuggets of coal into the fiery caverns the dying fire had made. A hiss, for the coal was damp after recent rain, and, for a moment, the glow on her face and hair darkened, then blazed up again.

'We seem to keep missing each other,' she said.

'You mean we're kept apart.'

That amazing hair, he thought. Even now, when it was all brushed and tamed for bed, he could see five or six different shades of copper, auburn, bronze, even a strand of pure gold that looked as if it must belong to somebody else.

She turned to look at him. 'It's her house, Billy.'

'Have I said anything?'

The firelight, gilding her face, disguised the munitions-factory yellow of her skin.

'We could get married by special licence,' he said. 'At least I suppose we could, I don't know how long it takes.'

'No, we couldn't.'

No, he thought, because after the war things'll be different, I could be getting on in the world, I might not want to be saddled with a wife from Beale Street. I have to be protected from myself. Sarah had a great sense of honour. About as much use to a woman as a jock-strap, he'd have thought, but there it was, Sarah was saddled with it. 'I love you, Sarah Lumb.'

'I love you, Billy Prior.'

She leant back, and he unbuttoned her night-dress, pushing it off her shoulders so that the side of one heavy breast was etched in trembling gold. He slid to the floor beside her and took her in his arms, feeling her tense against him. 'It's all right, it's all right.'

And all he wanted, at that moment, was to hide his face between her breasts and shut out the relentless ticking of the clock. But a voice above shouted, 'Sarah? Cynthia? Time you were asleep.'

'I'll have to go.'

'All right.'

But his hands refused to loosen their grip, and she had to pull herself away.

'Look, tomorrow night she goes to the spuggies. I'll tell her I've got a headache, and see if I can stay here.'

Next morning, after they'd all gone to work, he went upstairs to Sarah's room, exhausted after another bad night measured by the chiming of the clock. He needed to lie in the bed where Sarah slept, to wrap himself in these stained sheets, for even in this fanatically clean household the girls' skins sloughed off, staining the sheets yellow, and no amount of washing would get the stains out. He didn't mind. He would lie happily here, in the trough made by her body during the night, smelling the faint smell of lavender and soap.

On the bedside table was a photograph of himself,

taken when he was first commissioned. Unformed schoolboy face. Had he ever been as young as that? Undressed and in bed, he squinted at the half-drawn curtains, wondering if it was worth the effort of getting up to close them. No, he decided, he would simply turn his back to the light.

He turned over, and for a second closed his eyes, his brain not immediately interpreting what in that brief glance he had seen. Then he sat up. On the dresser stood a photograph of a young man in uniform, a private's uniform. Not Cynthia's husband – he knew his face from wedding groups. He got out of bed and went to look. Johnny, of course. Who else? Sarah's first fiancé.

The usual inanely smiling face half whited out by the sun. Behind him, a few feet of unbombed France. And why should he begrudge this? *Because I thought I'd taken his place.* He hadn't even thought it, he'd just assumed it. She'd talked only once about Johnny and then she'd been drunk on the port he'd been plying her with to get her knickers off. Loos. That was it. Gas blown back over the British lines. He peered again at the unknown face. The whiting out seemed almost to be an unintended symbol of the oblivion into which we all go. Last night, he'd wondered what colour Sarah's skin had been under the jaundice produced by the chemicals she worked with. This man had known. He'd known *this* Sarah – picking up a snapshot – this happy, slightly plump, hoydenish girl struggling to keep her skirts down on the boat-swing. What you noticed in Sarah now was the high rounded forehead, the prominent cheekbones, the bright, cool amused gaze. Always the sense of something being held back. He'd been looking all along at a face scoured out by grief, and he'd never known it till now.

'Nice walk in the fresh air,' Ada said, spearing black felt with a hat-pin. 'Just the thing for a headache.'

'I won't be in the fresh air, Mam. That room gets awfully stuffy, you know.'

Ada bent down, thrusting her face into her daughter's. 'Sarah, go and get your coat.'

Sarah looked at Billy and shrugged slightly.

'I'll come too,' he said, standing up.

'Are you sure?' Ada asked. 'The spuggies aren't everybody's cup of tea.'

'Wouldn't miss it for the world.'

They walked down the street together, Ada leading the way, sweeping along in her black skirt, for in the matter of skirt length she made no concessions to the present day. She glided along as if on invisible casters.

'I suppose she does know contacting the dead's a heresy?' Billy asked. 'The Vicar wouldn't like it.'

'Oh, she doesn't believe in it. She only goes for the night out.'

The meeting was held above a shop that sold surgical appliances, a range of products whose advertising is necessarily discreet. The window, lined with red and green crêpe paper left over from Christmas, contained nothing but a picture of a white-haired man swinging his granddaughter above his head.

They went up a narrow staircase into a tiny room. A piano, a table with a vase of flowers, five or six rows of chairs, net curtains whose shadows tattooed skin. They couldn't find four seats together and so Prior found himself sitting behind Sarah.

'How's your headache, Sarah?' Ada asked.

'Bit better, thank you, Mam.'

How's your ballsache, Billy? Bloody awful, thank you, Ma.

A man walked up and stood on the rostrum, looking carefully round the room. Counting the penny contributions to tea and biscuits? Assessing the general level of credulity? Or was he perhaps not a rogue at all but simply mad? No, not mad. A small, self-satisfied man with brown teeth.

Prior followed his gaze round the room, as the blinds were drawn down, shutting out the sun. Women, mostly in black, a scattering of men, all middle aged or older, except one, whose hands and face twitched uncontrollably. Too many widows. Too many mothers looking for contact with lost sons – and this was an area where they'd all joined up together. Whole streets of them, going off in a day. And this man, smoothing down his thin hair, announcing the number of the hymn, had known them all – birthmarks, nicknames, funny little habits – he knew exactly what every woman in this room

77

wanted to hear. Fraud, Prior thought, and that he deceived himself made it no better.

Angels of Jesus, Angels of Light
Singing to we-elcome the pilgrims of the night.

They sat down with the usual coughs, chair scrapings, tummy rumbles, and he stood in front of them, establishing the silence, deepening it.

At last he was ready. Their loved ones were with them, he said, they were present in this room. The messages started coming. First a description, then a flicker of the eyes in the direction of the woman whose husband or son he had been describing, then the message. Anodyne messages. They were having a whale of a time, it seemed, on the other side, beyond this vale of tears, singing hymns, rejoicing in the Lamb, casting down their golden crowns around the glassy sea. Ah, yes, Prior wanted to ask, but how's the fucking?

Then, without warning, the twitching man stood up and started to speak. Not words. A gurgling rush of sound like the overflow of a drainpipe, and yet with inflections, pauses, emphases, everything that speech contains except meaning. People turned towards him, watching the sounds jerk out of him, as he stood with thrown-back head and glazed eyes. The man on the rostrum was wearing a forced, sickly smile. One hysteric upstaged by another. I'd take the pair of you on, Prior thought.

He touched Sarah's shoulder. 'I can't stand any more of this. I'll wait outside.'

He ran downstairs, then crossed the street and slipped into the alley opposite, positioning himself midway between two stinking midden holes. He lit a cigarette and thought *glossolalia*. 'A spiritual gift of no intrinsic significance, unless the man possessing it can interpret what he receives in a way that tends to the edification of the faithful.' Father Mackenzie, preparing him for Confirmation, when he was ... eleven years old? Twelve? What a teacher the man was – in or out of his cassock.

From his vantage point, watching like a stranger, he saw Sarah come out and look up and down the empty road.

'Sarah.'

She ran across, face pale beneath the munitions-factory yellow. 'What happened?'

'Nothing. I couldn't stand it, that's all.' A pause. 'We have to die, we don't have to worship it.'

They stood together, looking up and down the street, which was dotted here and there with puddles of recent rain. Fitful gleams of sunlight.

'I'm not going back in.'

'No.'

She waited, still worried.

'We could go back home,' she said.

'Have you got a key?'

'Yes.'

They stared at each other.

'Come on,' he said, grabbing her arm.

They ran along the shining street, splashing

through puddles, Sarah's hair coming loose in a cascade of pins, then down an alley where white sheets bellied and snapped, shirt-sleeves caught them, wet cotton stung their faces and necks. They arrived at the door red-faced, Sarah's hair hanging in rat's-tails down her back.

She rattled the key in the lock, while he stood looking back the way they'd come, half expecting to see Ada hurtling towards them on her Widow-of-Windsor casters. They half fell into the passage, and he ran towards the stairs. 'No,' she said. No, he thought. The front room, then. He made to pull the curtains across. 'No, don't do that, they'll think somebody's dead. Behind the sofa.' He was already on his knees in front of her, his hands under her skirt, groping for the waistband of her drawers, pulling them down, casting them aside, he didn't care where they fell. At the last moment he thought, This isn't going to work. They'd had to leave the front door open – it would be impossible to explain why it was locked – but the thought of Ada Lumb looking down at your bare arse was enough to give a brass monkey the wilts.

'Careful,' Sarah said, as he went in.

But he's always careful, always prepared – though never prepared for the surge of joy he feels now. He's like some aquatic animal, an otter, returning to its burrow, greeting its mate nose to nose, curling up, safe, warm, dark, wet. His mind shrinks to a point that listens for footsteps, but his cock swells, huge and blind, filling the world. His thrusts deepen and quicken, but then he forces himself to pull back, to keep them shallow, a butterfly fluttering that he knows she likes. Her hands come up and grasp his buttocks – always a moment of danger – and for a while he has to stop altogether, hanging there, mouth open. Then, cautiously, he starts again. Cords stand out in her neck, her belly tightens, the fingers clutching his arse are claws now. She groans, and he feels the movement of muscles in her belly. Another groan, a cry, and now it's impossible to stop, every thrust as irresistible as the next breath to a drowning man. She raises her legs higher, inviting him deeper, and he tries not to hear the desperation in her gasps, the disappointment in her final cry, as he spills himself into her.

'Yes?' he gasps, as soon as he can speak.

'No.'

Oh God. He drives himself on, thrusting away in a frictionless frenzy, his knob a point of fire, feeling her teeter teeter on the brink, and then at last at last tip over, fall, clutching and throbbing round his shrinking cock till he cries out in pain. Oh, but she's there, she's laughing, he hears her laughter deep in his chest.

Only his groin's wet, too wet. He lifted himself off her and looked down. Spunk, beaten stiff as egg-white, streaked their hair, flecks of foam on a horse's muzzle, spume blown back from the breaking wave, but to him it meant one thing. The johnny –

unfortunate word in the circumstances – was still inside Sarah. He hooked it out, and they stared at it.

Sarah felt inside. 'I think I'm all right,' she said. 'It's all outside.'

No oiled casters, but a firm tread approached the house. He flung the rubber into the fire, a million or so Billies and Sarahs perishing in a gasp of flame. Small bloody comfort if another million were still inside her. She pulled her skirts down and sat, sweating and desperate, in her mother's chair. He was about to sit down himself when he caught sight of her drawers thrown across the family Bible, one raised leg drawing a decent veil over Job and his boils. He snatched them up and stuffed them down the neck of his tunic, which left him no time for his flies. He picked up the Bible and sat with it in his lap.

'Well,' Ada said. 'What happened to you?'

Sarah said, 'Billy started thinking about a friend of his, Mam.'

Prior sat with his head on one hand, a passable imitation of David mourning Jonathan.

Ada sniffed. 'I see you've not thought to put the kettle on, our Sarah. It's a true saying in this life, if you want anything doing do it yourself.'

She went into the kitchen. Cynthia, glancing timidly from one to the other, sat down on the edge of the sofa. Billy pulled Sarah's drawers out of his tunic and threw them across to her. Cynthia squealed, bunching her clothes between her legs like a little girl afraid of wetting herself. Sarah calmly stood up and put the drawers on, while Prior fumbled with buttons beneath the Bible.

Ada came back into the room. 'You missed a good show,' she said. 'Mrs Roper had to be carried out. Still, no doubt you've been better employed.' She indicated the Bible.

'I was just trying to find the bit about the war-horse to show Sarah. But it's all right, I know it off by heart.' He looked straight at Ada. '*He paweth in the valley and rejoiceth in his strength: he goeth on to meet the armed men. He mocketh at fear, and is not affrighted; neither turneth he back from the sword. He saith among the trumpets, Ha, ha; and he smelleth the battle afar off, the thunder of the captains, and the shouting.*'

He got up and replaced the Bible, aware of three faces gawping at him. An odd moment. 'And now if you don't mind,' he said, 'I think I'd like to lie down.'

Sarah was allowed to go to the railway station with him unaccompanied. They stood on the empty plat-form, exhausted mentally and physically, obliged to cherish these last moments together, both secretly, guiltily wanting it to be over.

He picked up her hand and kissed the ring. 'Don't worry, Sarah.'

'I'm not worried.' She smiled. 'This time next year.'

He hadn't thought about the actual marriage at all,

once she'd made it clear she didn't want a quick wedding. Next year was a lifetime away. Perhaps even a bit more. He watched a pigeon walk along the edge of the platform, raw feet clicking on the concrete. 'Come on,' he said. 'Let's walk along.'

They stopped under the shelter of the roof, for there was a fine rain blowing. White northern light filtered through sooty glass. Sarah's face pinched with cold.

'Write as soon as you get there,' she said.

'I'll write from London. I'll write on the train if you like.'

She smiled and shook her head. 'I'm glad you told your mam anyway.'

'She was delighted.'

She was horrified.

– *Marrying a factory girl not that it matters of course as long as you're happy but I'd've thought you could have done a bit better for yourself than that.*

His father was incredulous.

– *Married? You?*

– *Oscar Wilde was married, Dad,* Prior had not been able to resist saying.

But then his father had come to the station to see him off – first time in four years – *and* he'd to get out of bed to do it, because he was on nights, *and* he was wearing his Sunday suit, *and* he'd shaved, *and* he was sober. Jesus Christ, Prior had thought, all we need is the wreath.

A small hard pellet of dismay lodged in his throat.

Premonition? *No-o*, nothing so portentous. A slight sense of pushing his luck, perhaps. This was the fourth time, and four was one too many.

'I expect they'll invite you over.'

Sarah smiled. 'I think I'll wait till you get back.'

He glanced covertly at his watch. Where was the bloody train? And then he saw it, in the distance, crawling doubtfully along, trailing its plume of steam. No sound yet, though as he stepped closer to the edge of the platform he felt or sensed a vibration in the rails. He turned to face Sarah, blocking her view of the train.

She was looking up at the rafters. 'Have you seen them?'

He followed her gaze and saw that every rafter was lined with pigeons. 'The warmth, I suppose,' he said vaguely.

The roar of the approaching train startled the birds. They rose as one, streaming out from under the glass roof in a great flapping and beating of wings, wheeling, banking, swooping, turning, a black wave against the smoke-filled sky. Prior and Sarah watched, open-mouthed, drunk on the sight of so much freedom, their linked hands slackening, able, finally, to think of nothing, as the train steamed in.

SIX

After tea he took Kath's photograph album up to her room. He usually brought snapshots of family and friends with him on these visits, because he knew how much pleasure they gave her. She was sitting up in bed, faded brown hair tied back by a blue ribbon, a pink bed jacket draped around her shoulders. Blue and pink: the colours of the nursery. He took the tray off her lap and gave her the album and the photographs.

She seized on a group of staff at the Empire Hospital. 'You've got your usual I-don't-want-to-be-photographed expression,' she said, holding it up to the light.

'Well, I didn't.'

She was already busy pasting glue on to the back. 'Is it true the natives think the camera steals their souls?'

'Some of them. The sensible ones.'

She pressed her handkerchief carefully around the

edges of the photograph, catching the seepage of glue. 'It's a good one of Dr Head.'

'Oh, Henry isn't worried, he hasn't got a soul.'

'*Will.*'

He looked at the tray. 'You haven't eaten much.'

'I'm glad Ethel's having a break. It's been a shocking year.'

Ramsgate had been bombed heavily, a great many civilians, mainly women and children, killed. As a result Kath's health, which had long given cause for concern, had dramatically deteriorated. Ethel, who'd looked after their father in his old age, and then after this invalid younger sister, had begun to show signs of strain herself, and the brothers had decided something must be done. A holiday was out of the question, ruled out by Ethel herself – she could not and would not go – but she *had* agreed to stay with friends for a long weekend.

'I think that's the car now,' Rivers said. 'I'd better get the suitcase down.'

He found Ethel in the hall, pinning on her hat.

'Now,' she said, unable to let go, 'you've got the telephone number?'

'Yes.'

'You're sure you've got it?'

'Yes.' He pushed her gently towards the door.

'No, *listen*, Will. If you're worried, don't hesitate, call the doctor.'

'Ethel, I *am* a doctor.'

'No, I mean a *proper* doctor.'

He was still smiling as he went back upstairs.

'Is she gone?'

'Yes, I had to push her out of the door, but she's gone. Have you finished sticking them in?'

He took the album from her and began turning the pages, pausing at a photograph of himself and the other members of the Torres Straits expedition. Barefoot, bare-armed, bearded, sun-tanned, wearing a collection of spectacularly villainous hats, they looked for all the world like a low-budget production of *The Pirates of Penzance*. The flower of British anthropology, he thought, God help us. He turned a few more pages, stopping at a snapshot from his days in Heidelberg. What on earth made him think those side whiskers were a good idea?

'I knew you'd stop there,' Katharine said. 'It's her, isn't it? The stout one.'

'Alma? Of course it isn't.' His sisters had teased him mercilessly at the time, because he'd happened to be standing next to Alma in a snapshot. 'Anyway, she wasn't stout, she was ... comfortable.'

'She was stout. We really did think you were going to marry her, you know. She was the only woman we ever saw you with.'

'That's not true either. Remember all the young ladies mother used to invite to tea?'

'I remember you sloping off upstairs to get away from them. You were just like Mr Dodgson. He used to do that.'

Kath sometimes combined with childlike innocence a child's sharpness of perception.

'*Like Dodgson?* God forbid.'

'You didn't like him, did you?'

He hesitated. 'No.'

'You were jealous. You and Charles.'

'Yes, I think we were. Ah, *this* is the girl I'm
looking for,' he said, holding up a photograph of a
little girl in a white dress. Even in faded sepia it was
possible to tell what an exceptionally beautiful child
she'd been.

Light from the standard lamp fell on the side of
Dodgson's face as he opened the book.

'S-shouldn't we wait f-for K-K-K-Kath?' he asked,
the name clotting on his tongue.

Sitting on the sofa beside Charles, Will thought,
That's because it's the same sound as hard *c*. *C*
was Dodgson's worst consonant. *F* and *m* were
his.

'No, I think we should start,' his father said. 'It's
not fair to keep everybody waiting, just because
Kath's late.'

'She'll be here soon,' Mother said. 'Her stomach's
a good clock.'

'Aren't you w-w-w-w-w-woorr . . .?'

'Not really. She knows she mustn't leave the
grounds.'

Will intercepted a glance between his parents.
Mother shouldn't have completed Mr Dodgson's

sentence for him like that. You were supposed to let people flounder, no matter how long it took.

Mr Dodgson stammered less when he read. And why was that? Because he knew the words so well he didn't have to think about them? Or because, although his voice was loud, he was really just reading to Ethel, who sat curled up in the crook of his arm, where she could see the pictures? He never stammered much when he was talking to the girls. Or was it because these were *his* words, and he was determined to get them out, no matter what? It certainly wasn't because he was thinking about the movements of his tongue, which was what father said you should do.

'The rabbit hole,' Mr Dodgson read, or rather recited, for he was not looking at the page but at the top of Ethel's head, 'went straight on like a tunnel for some way, and then dipped suddenly down, so suddenly that Alice had not a moment to think about stopping herself before she found herself falling down a very deep –'

Kath burst in, hot, dirty, dishevelled, trailing her hat by its long blue ribbon, raspberry stains round her mouth, grubby hands streaked with cuckoo spit. She went straight to Mr Dodgson and gave him a bunch of flowers whose stalks had wilted in the heat and flopped over the back of her hand.

He took them from her and sat looking stupid, not knowing where to put them, when his attention was caught. 'Look,' he said, 'you've g-g-got a l-l-l-ladybird in your h-hair.'

Kath stood, breathing through her mouth with concentration, as he teased the strands of hair apart and persuaded the insect on to the tip of his finger. He showed it to her, then carefully stood up, meaning to carry it to the window, but the scarlet shards parted, the black wings spread, and the insect sailed out, a dark speck on the blue air.

Dodgson sat down, drew Katharine on to his lap, folded his other arm round Ethel again, and picked up the book.

'– *well*,' he said, and everybody laughed.

'Do you remember how he hated snakes?' Kath said, leaning back against the pillows with the sunlight on her greying hair.

'Yes, I remember.'

He was thinking that the whole course of Kath's life had been constriction into a smaller and smaller space. As children they'd both had a hundred acres of safe woods and fields to roam in, but from that point on *his* life had expanded: medical school, round the world as a ship's doctor, Germany, the Torres Straits, India, Australia, the Solomon Islands, the New Hebrides. And over the same period the little girl who'd rambled all day through woods and fields had become the younger of the two Miss Rivers, scrutinized by her father's parishioners, the slightest breach of decorum noted, and then, after father's retirement, a small house in Ramsgate, deteriorating health, confinement to the house, then to the bedroom, then to the bed. And yet she was no more intrinsically neurasthenic than he was himself. But a good mind must have something to feed on, and hers, deprived of other nourishment, had fed on itself.

He said slowly, 'I think what I remember most is endless croquet.' Oh God, he remembered, hours and hours of it, a vast red sun hanging above the trees, Dodgson's body forming a hoop round Kath's, his hands enclosing hers, the click of mallets on balls, and mother's voice drifting across the lawn asking how much longer were they going to be? It was time for Kath to come in. 'Mathematical croquet,' Rivers said. 'Nobody could win.'

'I used to win.'

'He helped you cheat.'

'Yes.' A faint smile. 'I know he did.'

Once, on the river, Dodgson had tried to pin up Kath's skirts so she could paddle. He'd done it often enough before, indeed he carried safety-pins in his lapels specifically for the purpose, but this time she'd pushed him away. Some intensity in his gaze? Some quality in his touch? Their mother had spoken sharply to her, but Dodgson had said, 'No, leave her alone.'

'It's a pity we lost his letters,' Rivers said.

'Oh, and the drawings. There was a whole crate of things went missing. I'm sure that painting of Uncle Will went at the same time –'

'I don't remember that.'

'Yes, you do.'

'Where was it?'

'At the top of the stairs. You couldn't put it in the drawing-room, it was too horrible.'

'What was it of?'

'Uncle William having his leg cut off. And there was somebody waiting with a sort of cauldron full of hot tar ready to pour it over the stump.'

'Are you sure?'

'You didn't like it. When we all went downstairs in the morning I used to see you not looking at it. You were like this.' She turned her head to one side.

'Well, you have surprised me.'

A modestly triumphant smile. 'I remember more than you do.'

Though, even as she spoke, he had a faint, very faint, recollection of Father lifting him up to look at something. A curious exposed feeling at the nape of his neck. 'Father tried very hard with Charles and me. Didn't he?'

'You more than Charles.'

'Ah, well, yes, I was the guinea-pig, wasn't I? The first child always is.' A greater bitterness in his voice than he knew how to account for. He brushed it aside. 'I'll make us some cocoa, shall I? And then I think you should try and get some sleep.'

— *Do you remember how he hated snakes?*

— *Yes, I remember.*

That's the trouble, Rivers thought, taking off his shirt in the spare bedroom that had once been his father's study, I remember her childhood better than my own. Though another person's life, observed from outside, always has a shape and definition that one's own life lacks.

It was odd he couldn't remember that picture, when Kath, ten years younger, remembered it so clearly. He'd certainly have been shown it, many many times. He was named after William Rivers of the *Victory*, who, as a young midshipman, had shot the man who shot Lord Nelson. That was the family legend anyway. And the great man, dying, had not indulged in any effete nonsense about kissing Hardy, nor had he entrusted Lady Hamilton to the conscience of a grateful nation. *No*, his last words had been, 'Look after young Will Rivers for me.' And young Will Rivers had needed looking after. He'd been wounded in the mouth and leg, and the leg had had to be amputated. Without an anaesthetic, since there were no anaesthetics, except rum. And then hot tar to cauterize the spurting stump. My God, it was a wonder any of them survived. And throughout the ordeal – family legend again – he had not once cried out. He'd survived, married, had children, become Warden of Greenwich Hospital. There was a portrait bust of him there, in the Painted Hall.

Now *that* he did remember being taken to see. Was that the occasion on which his father had lifted him up to look? No, he'd have been eight or nine.

And then he remembered. Quite casually, a bubble breaking on the surface. He'd had his hair cut, he'd just been breeched, yes, that was it, his neck felt funny, and so did his legs. And he was crying. Yes, it was all coming back. He'd embarrassed his father in the barber's shop by howling his head off. Bits of him were being cut off, bits of him were dropping on to the floor. His father shushed him, and when that didn't work, slapped his leg. He gasped with shock, filled his lungs with air, and howled louder. So being shown the picture was a lesson? You don't behave like *that*, you behave like *this*. '*He* didn't cry,' his father had said, holding him up. '*He didn't make a sound.*'

And I've been stammering ever since, Rivers thought, inclined to see the funny side. Though what had it meant – Trafalgar, the Napoleonic wars – to a four-year-old for whom a summer's day was endless? Nothing, it could have meant nothing. Or, worse, it had meant something fearfully simple. The same name, the slapped leg, being told not to cry. Had he perhaps looked at the picture and concluded that this was what happened to you if your name was William Rivers?

He'd avoided looking at it, Kath said, even turning his head away so that he could not glimpse it by mistake as he went past. Had he also deliberately suppressed the visual image of it, making it impossible for himself to see it in his mind's eye? Prior, told that Rivers attributed his almost total lack of visual memory to an event in his childhood that he had succeeded in forgetting, had said brutally, 'You were raped or beaten . . . Whatever it was, you put your mind's eye out rather than have to go on seeing it. Is that what happened, or isn't it?' Yes, Rivers had been obliged to admit, though he'd argued very strongly for a less dramatic interpretation of events. It could have been something quite trivial, he'd said, though terrifying to a child. Something as simple as the fearsome shadow of a dressing-gown on the back of the nursery door. Small children are not like adults, he'd insisted. What terrifies them may seem trivial to us.

Was this *the* suppressed memory? He didn't know. Was it trivial? Well, yes, in a way, compared with Prior's lurid imaginings. A smack on the leg, a lesson in manliness from an over-conscientious but loving father. It's a long way from sadistic beatings or sexual assault. And yet it wasn't as trivial as it seemed at first. That silence – for him now that was the centre of the picture – not the blood, not the knife, but that resolutely clenched mouth. Every day of his working life he looked at twitching mouths that had once been clenched. Go on, he said, though rarely in so many words, cry. It's all right to grieve. Break-down's nothing to be ashamed of – the pressures were intolerable. But, also, stop crying. Get up on your feet. Walk. He both distrusted that silence and endorsed it, as he was bound to do, he thought, being his father's son.

He went to Greenwich by train, visited the portrait bust in the Painted Hall, then continued his journey by steamer, arriving at Westminster steps in the late afternoon. The underground was crowded, he couldn't find a taxi, and by the time he turned the corner of Holford Road Prior was already there, standing on the steps. 'Have you knocked?' Rivers asked.

'No, I saw you coming. Been at the hospital?'

'No, I've just got back from Ramsgate.' He fitted his key into the lock. 'Now if we tiptoe across the hall . . .'

Prior smiled, having encountered Rivers's landlady many times in the past.

'All clear,' Rivers said.

They walked upstairs side by side, Rivers noticing how easily Prior was breathing. Sometimes, during the past summer, he'd listened to Prior's step on these stairs and counted the pauses. He'd never gone out on to the top landing to greet Prior as he did with all his other patients because he knew how intolerable he would find it to be seen fighting for breath. But now his chest was remarkably clear, a reflection perhaps of the satisfaction he felt at going back to France. Rivers opened the door of his rooms, and stood aside to let Prior enter.

Somehow or other he had to prevent this meeting becoming a confrontation, as consultations with Prior still tended to do. Prior would enjoy the skirmish at the time – there was nothing he liked better – but he'd regret it later. 'Well, sit yourself down,' Rivers said, taking Prior's coat and pointing to a chair by the fire. 'How are you?'

'Quite well. Chest works. Tongue works.'

'Nightmares?'

'Hmm . . . a few. I had one where the faces on the revolver targets – you know, horrible snarling baby-eating boche – turned into the faces of people I love. But only after I'd pulled the trigger, so there was nothing I could do about it. 'Fraid I killed you every time.'

'Ah, so it isn't a *bad* nightmare, then?'

They smiled at each other. Rivers thought Prior was entirely unaware of what he'd said, though that was always a dangerous assumption to make about Prior. Perhaps because he'd recently been thinking about his own father Rivers was more than usually aware of the strong father–son element in his relationship with Prior. He had no son; Prior utterly rejected his natural father. 'Oh, by the way, congratulations on your engagement.'

Hmm, Prior thought. Charles Manning's congratulations had also been brief, though in his case the brevity might be excused, since he'd had to take Prior's cock out of his mouth to be able to say anything at all. 'Thank you.'

'Have you fixed a date?'

'Next August. We met in August, we got engaged in August, so . . .'

'And when do you leave for France?'

'Tonight. I'm glad to be going.'

'Yes.'

Prior smiled. 'Do *you* think I'm ready to go back?'

A slight hesitation. 'I think I'd be happier if you did another twelve weeks' home service. Which would still,' he persisted across Prior's interruptions, 'get you back to France by the end of November.'

'Why?'

'You know why. Two months ago you were having memory lapses. Rather bad ones actually. Anyway this is purely hypothetical. Wasn't my decision –'

Prior leant forward. 'I was afraid you'd write.'

'It never occurred to me anybody would think of sending you back.'

'I think the MO was against it. Well, that was my impression anyway. How would I know? As for the Board, well, they wanted to send me back. I wanted to go.'

'What did they ask you about? Nerves?'

'No, not mentioned. They don't believe in shell-shock. You'd be surprised how many army Medical Boards don't.'

Rivers snorted. 'Oh, I don't think I would. Anyway, you're going back. You've got what you wanted.'

'At the moment I can't wait to see the back of England.'

'Any particular reason?'

'It's nothing really. I just had my fur rubbed up the wrong way.' He hesitated. 'Manning took me to meet Robert Ross. I don't know whether you've met him? Through Sassoon?'

'Briefly.'

'I liked him, he was charming – I wasn't equally keen on some of his friends.'

Rivers waited.

'One in particular. Apparently he'd been stood up by his boyfriend – he'd been expecting an amorous weekend – and the poor chap had decided it wasn't worth the train fare from Leeds. And this man – Birtwhistle, his name is – was saying, "Of course one can't rely on them. Their values are totally different from ours. They're a different species, really. The WCs." Smirk, smirk.'

Rivers looked puzzled.

'Working classes. Water-closets. The men who're getting their ballocks shot off so he can go on being the lily on the dung heap. God, they make me sick.'

'I'm sure you more than held your own.'

'No, I didn't, that's what bothers me. It all got tangled up with being a guest and being polite. To Ross, of course, not him. Anyway I decided to give this prat a run for his money so we adjourned upstairs afterwards.'

'You and Manning?'

'No, me and Birtwhistle. Birtwhistle and I.'

'It doesn't sound much like a punishment.'

'Oh, it was. Nothing like *sexual* humiliation, Rivers. Nobody ever forgets that.'

Rivers looked into the trustless eyes, and thought,

My God, I wouldn't want to cross you. Though he had crossed him many times, in the course of therapy, *and* refused more than one invitation to 'adjourn upstairs'.

'I just wish your last evening had been pleasanter.'

Prior shrugged. 'It was all right. It just . . . he happens to represent everything in England that *isn't* worth fighting for. Which made him a rather bracing companion.' He glanced at his watch. 'I'd better be going. I'm catching the midnight train.'

Rivers hesitated. 'Please don't think because I *personally* would have recommended another three months in England that I don't have every confidence in your ability to . . . to . . .'

'Do my duty to King and country.'

'Yes.'

'Rivers, you don't think I should be going back at all.'

Rivers hesitated. 'The Board at Craiglockhart recommended permanent home service and that wasn't because of your nerves, it was on the basis of your asthma alone. I haven't seen anything to make me change my mind.'

Prior looked at him, smiled, and slapped him on both arms. 'I've got to go.'

Rivers said slowly, as he went to get Prior's coat, 'Do you remember saying something to me once about the the the ones who go back b-being the *real* test cases? From the point of view of finding out whether a particular therapy works?'

'Yes, I remember.' Another smile. 'I was getting at you.'

'You always were. Well, it just occurs to me you're actually rather better equipped than most people to observe that process. I think you have great powers of detachment.'

'"Cold-blooded little bastard,"' Prior translated, then thought for a moment. 'You're giving me a football to kick across, aren't you? You remember that story? The Suffolk's kicking a football across No Man's Land when the whistles blew on the Somme? Bloody mad.'

'No, the battle was mad. The football was sane. Whoever ordered them to do that was a very good psychologist.'

'*Ah!*'

'But I know what you mean. It's become the kind of incident one can't take seriously any more. Only I'm not sure that's right, you see. I suppose what one *should* be asking is whether an ideal becomes invalid because the people who hold it are betrayed.'

'If holding it makes them into naïve idiots, *yes.*'

'Were they?'

'If they were, I can't talk. I'm going back.'

Rivers smiled. 'So you don't want my football?'

'On the contrary, I think it's a brilliant idea. I'll send you the half-time score.'

Rivers handed him his greatcoat, examining it first. 'I'm impressed.'

'So you should be at the price.' Prior started to put

it on. 'Do you know you can get these with scarlet silk linings?'

'Army greatcoats?'

'Yes. Saw one in the Café Royal. On the back of one of my old intelligence colleagues. Quite a startling effect when he crossed his legs, *subtle*, you know, like a baboon's bottom. Apparently he's supposed to sit there and "attract the attention of anti-war elements".'

'Was he?'

'He was attracting attention. I don't know what their views on the war were. Another thing that made me glad to be getting out of it.' He held out his hand. 'Don't come down.'

Rivers took him at his word, but went through to the bedroom window and looked out, lifting the curtain an inch to one side. Miss Irving's voice, a laughing farewell, and then Prior appeared, foreshortened, running down the steps.

On Vao there was a custom that when a bastard was born some leading man on the island adopted the child and brought him up as his own. The boy called him father, and grew up surrounded by love and care and then, when he reached puberty, he was given the honour, as befitted the son of a great man, of leading in the sacrificial pig, one of the huge-tusked boars in which the wealth of the people was measured. He was given new bracelets, new necklaces, a new penis wrapper and then, in front of the entire community, all of whom knew what was about to happen, he led the pig to the sacrificial stone, where his father waited with upraised club. And, as the boy drew near, he brought the club down and crushed his son's skull.

In one of his father's churches, St Faith's, at Maidstone, the window to the left of the altar shows Abraham with the knife raised to slay his son, and, below the human figures, a ram caught in the thicket by his horns. The two events represented the difference between savagery and civilization, for in the second scenario the voice of God is about to forbid the sacrifice, and will be heeded. He had knelt at that altar rail for years, Sunday after Sunday, receiving the chalice from his father's hands.

Perhaps, Rivers thought, watching Prior's head bob along behind the hedge and disappear from view, it was because he'd been thinking so much about fathers and sons recently that the memory of the two sacrifices had returned, but he wished this particular memory had chosen another moment to surface.

PART TWO

SEVEN

29 August 1918

Bought this in a stationer's just off Fleet Street quite a long time ago. I've been carrying it round with me ever since unused, mainly because it's so grand. I bought it for the marbled covers and the thick creamy pages and ever since then the thick creamy pages have been saying, Piss off, what could *you* possibly write on *us* that would be worth reading? It's a marvellous shop, a real old-fashioned stationer's. Stationers', second-hand bookshops, ironmongers'. Feel a great need at the moment to concentrate on small pleasures. If the whole of one's life can be summoned up and held in the palm of one hand, *in the living moment*, then time means nothing. World without end, Amen.

Load of crap. Facts are what we need, man. Facts.

Arrived in London to find no porters, no taxis, and the hotels full. Charles Manning on the platform (the train was so late I was sure he'd've gone home), offering, as a solution, the room he rents in Half

Moon Street, 'for the nights when he works late at the office and doesn't want to disturb the household'. Oh, c'mon, Charles, I wanted to say. It's *me*, remember? I was all for trudging round a few more hotels, but he was limping badly and obviously in pain *and* pissed off with me for going back when I could have been comfortably established in the Min of Mu chasing bits of paper across a desk, like him. (He'd go back to France tomorrow if they'd have him.)

When we got to Half Moon Street we went straight upstairs and he produced a bottle of whisky. Not bad (but not what he drinks himself either) and I waited for him to do what everybody else would do in the circumstances and collect the rent. He didn't, of course. I'm plagued with honourable people. I thought, Oh, for Christ's sake, if you haven't got the gumption to ask for it bloody do without. I was feeling tired and sticky and wanted a bath. After ten minutes of swishing soapy water round my groin and whisky round my guts I started to feel better. I had a quiet consultation with myself in the bathroom mirror, all steamy and pink and conspiratorial, and went back in and said, Right let's be having you. Over the end of the bed. He likes being dominated, as people often do who've never had to raise their voice in their lives to get other people running after them.

Then we went out to dinner, came back, Charles stayed a while, long enough to introduce me to Ross – extraordinary man, rather Chinese-looking, and not just physically, a sense of a very old civilization. I shook his hand and I thought I'm shaking the hand that . . . Well, there *is* the connection with Wilde. And I felt at home in this rather beleaguered little community. Beleaguered, because Ross thinks he's going to be arrested, he thinks the utterly disgusting Pemberton Billing affair has given them *carte blanche* to go ahead and do it. He may be exaggerating the risk, he looks ill, he looks as if he goes to bed and broods, but one or two people there, including Manning, don't seem to rule out an arrest. A comfortable atmosphere in spite of it. Soldiers who aren't militarists, pacifists who aren't prigs, and *talking* to each other. Now *there's* a miracle.

But then – Birtwhistle. He's a don at Cambridge, very clever, apparently. Curiously, he actually prides himself on having a broader grasp of British society than the average person, i.e. he pokes working-class boys' bottoms. Might even be true, I suppose, though the heterosexual equivalent doesn't pride itself on broadening its social experience whenever it nips off for a knee-wobbler in Bethnal Green. Ah, but these are *relationships*, Birtwhistle would say. Did say. Lurve, no less. And yet he spoke of his working-class lover – his W C – in tones of utter contempt. And he didn't succeed in placing me, or not accurately enough. So much for the broader grasp. I played a rather cruel convoluted game with him afterwards. Which satisfied me a great deal at the time, but now I feel contaminated, as I wouldn't have done if I'd kicked him in the balls (which would also have been kinder).

Manning – after we'd had sex – became very strange. Great distances opened up. Partly because he hadn't intended it to happen – or didn't think he had – and partly just because I'm going back and he isn't. Two inches of sheet between us – *miles miles*. I was glad when he went and I'm even more glad he's not here now. Very few pleasures in sex are any match for a narrow bed and cool, clean sheets. (A post-coital reflection if ever I heard one.)

30 *August*

Collected my coat today. I'm not even going to write down how much it cost, but it's warm and light and it looks good, and I need all of that.

Mooched round the rest of the day doing nothing very much. Dinner at Half Moon Street in my room. Saw Rivers afterwards. Had made up my mind not to ask what he thought about my going back – and specifically not to ask if he thought I was fit – then asked anyway and was predictably irritated by the answer.

I had a very clear perception while we were talking – I suppose because I've been away for a while – that his power over people, the power to heal if you like, springs directly from some sort of wound or deformity in him. He has a lot of strengths, but he isn't working from strength. Difficult to say this without sounding patronizing, which isn't how I feel. In fact for me it's the best thing about him – well the only thing that makes him tolerable, actually – that he *doesn't* sit behind the desk implicitly setting himself up as some sort of standard of mental health. He once said to me half the world's work's done by hopeless neurotics, and I think he had himself in mind. And me.

Got to the station with an hour to spare and Manning showed up. I wished he hadn't but there he was and of course we had one of these awful station conversations. The ripples between those going out and those staying behind are so bloody awful the whole thing's best avoided. However, we got through it, looked at each other through the window with mutual relief and then away we went. Or I went.

Arrived here (Folkestone) in the middle of the night, exhausted. There's something about railway stations, and I've been in a lot of them recently. The goodbyes all get trapped under the roof and suck the oxygen out of the air. No other reason for me to feel like this.

Saturday, 31 August

Woke tired. But got up anyway, not wasting time – 'wasting time', 'killing time' start to be phrases you notice – lying in bed, and sat on the balcony for a while watching the sun come up and decided to do what people always think about doing, and then think again and go back to sleep: I decided to swim before breakfast. So down to the beach. Hovered on the shingle by the waterline, told myself not to be so feeble, etc., and plunged in. Water pearly grey, absolutely bloody freezing, but, after the first shock, total exhilaration. I stood for a while afterwards up to my knees, feeling the surge and suck round my legs, neither in the sea nor on the land. Marvellous. Still the slanting light of early morning. Worm casts on the beach very prominent, the sun casting vast shadows from little things, and I thought of the beach outside Edinburgh where I made love to Sarah for the first time. Went straight back and wrote to her. Then walked through town, giving myself small treats, chocolates, etc. and avoiding other officers.

Saw Hallet with his family, looking quite desperate. All of them, but I meant Hallet. Poor little bugger's had a station goodbye that's lasted for *days*. I waved and passed on.

On board

People playing cards below deck, but there's quite a heave on the sea, and I'd rather be out here watching it. Great bands of pale green in the wake, laced with thick foam, and terns hovering, riding rather – only the most fractional adjustment of their wings needed to keep them motionless. And they come quite close.

Watched the cliffs disappear. Tried to think of something worthy of the occasion and came up with: *The further out from England the nearer is to France*, and then couldn't get rid of the bloody thing, it just ran round and round my head.

Hallet came up and stood a few yards away, not wanting to intrude on what he took to be a fond farewell to the motherland. In the end I gave in, we sat down and talked. Full of idealism. I'd rather have had the Walrus and the Carpenter.

It's very obvious that Hallet's adopted me. Like one of those little pilot fish or the terns for that matter. He thinks because I've been out three times before I know what's going on. Seems a bright enough lad. I wonder how long it'll take him to work out that *nobody* knows what's going on?

Sunday, 1 September

Étaples marginally less brutal than I remember it, though still a squad of men passed me running the gauntlet of the canaries, who yelled abuse in their faces much as they always did. And you think, All right it has to be brutal – think what they're being toughened up *for* – but actually that misses the point. It's the *impersonality* that forms the biggest part of the sheer fucking nastiness of this place. Nobody knows anybody. You marshal men around – they don't know you, don't trust you (why should they?) and you don't invest anything in them.

Same feeling, in a milder form, between the officers. We sleep in dormitories, and it's the same feeling you get on big wards in hospitals – privacy sacrificed without intimacy being gained.

Hallet's in the next bed. He sat on his bed this evening and showed me a photograph of his girl – fiancée, I should say. His parents think he's too young to marry, which he fiercely objects to, pointing out that he's old enough for *this*. Of course I don't think he's old enough for *this* either, but I don't say so. Instead I told him I'd got engaged too and showed him a photograph of Sarah. And then we sat smiling at each other inanely, feeling like complete idiots. Well, I did.

Wednesday, 4 September

Time passes quickly here. Enough to do during the day, and a fair amount of free time. But the atmosphere's awful. The mess has scuffed no-colour lino – the colour of misery, if misery has a colour – and a big round table in the middle, covered with dog-eared copies of *Punch* and *John Bull*, exactly like a dentist's waiting-room. The same pervasive fear. The same reluctance to waste time on people you're probably never going to see again anyway.

I get out as often as I can. Walked miles today, great windswept sandy foothills, and a long line of stunted pines all leaning away from the sea.

Saturday, 7 September

Posted to the 2nd Manchesters. We leave tomorrow.

It's evening now, and everybody's scribbling away, telling people the news, or as much of the news as we're allowed to tell them. I look up and down the dormitory and there's hardly a sound except for pages being turned, and here and there a pen scratching. It's like this every evening. And not just letters either. Diaries. Poems. At least two would-be poets in this hut alone.

Why? you have to ask yourself. I think it's a way of claiming immunity. First-person narrators can't die, so as long as we keep telling the story of our own lives we're safe. Ha bloody fucking Ha.

EIGHT

Rivers turned to watch the sun swelling and reddening as it sank, a brutal, bloody disc, scored by steeples and factory chimneys, obscured by a haze of drifting brown and yellow smoke.

He'd come out to walk on Hampstead Heath because he was feeling ill, and needed to clear his head before settling down to an evening's work, but it wasn't helping. With every step he felt worse, muscles aching, throat sore, eyes stinging, skin clammy. By the time he got back to his lodgings, he'd decided to miss dinner and go straight to bed. He knocked on the door of Mrs Irving's private apartments, told her he wasn't feeling well and wouldn't be in to dinner, and glimpsed through the open door the portrait of her dead son that hung above the mantelpiece, with flowers beneath it and candlesticks on either side.

Going slowly upstairs, pausing frequently to lean on the banister, Rivers thought about what he'd just seen: the portrait, the flowers. A shrine. Not fundamentally different from the skull houses of Pa Na Gundu where he'd gone with Njiru. The same human impulse at work. Difficult to know what to make of these flashes of cross-cultural recognition. From a strictly professional point of view, they were almost meaningless, but then one didn't have such experiences as a disembodied anthropological intelligence, but as a man, and as a man one had to make some kind of sense of them.

Once in bed he started to shiver. The sheets felt cold against his hot legs. He slept and dreamt of the croquet lawn at Knowles Bank, his mother in a long white dress coming out to call the children in, the sun setting over the wood casting very long, fine shadows across the lawn. The shadows of the hoops were particularly long and fearful. He'd been awake for several minutes before he realized he was trying to remember the rules of mathematical croquet, as devised by Dodgson, and actually feeling *distressed* because he couldn't remember them. Then he realized that although he was now fully awake he could still see the lawn, which meant his temperature was very high. Always, in a high fever, his visual memory returned, giving him a secret, obscurely shameful pleasure in being ill. He wouldn't sleep again – he was far too hot – so he simply lay and let his newly opened mind's eye roam.

On the *Southern Cross*, on the voyage to Eddystone, he'd stood on deck, watching the pale green wake furrow the dark sea, reluctant to exchange the slight breeze for the stuffy heat below deck.

At one of the stops a group of natives got on, the men wearing cast-off European suits, the women floral-print dresses. A few of the women had naked breasts, but most were obviously missionized. A pathetic little remnant they looked, squatting there, part of the small army of uprooted natives who drifted from one island to the next, one mission station to the next, and belonged nowhere. At first sight all mission stations seemed to be surrounded by converts, and the uninitiated always assumed these were converts from *that* island. Only later did one become aware of this uprooted population, travelling from one station to the next, most of them from islands where the impact of western culture had been particularly devastating.

He squatted down beside them, and, as he expected, found enough knowledge of pidgin to make conversation possible. He'd devised a questionnaire that he used on occasions when it was necessary to extract the maximum amount of information quickly. The first question was always: Suppose you were lucky enough to find a guinea, with whom would you share it? This produced a list of names, names which he would then ask them to translate into kinship terms. And from there one could move to virtually any aspect of their society.

When he sensed they were getting tired he paid them their tobacco sticks and stood up to go, but then one of the women caught his arm and pulled him down again. Poking him playfully in the chest, she retrieved two words of English from her small store: 'Your turn.'

The questions were posed again and in the same order. When he told them that, since he was unmarried and had no children, he would not necessarily feel obliged to share his guinea with anybody, they at first refused to believe him. Had he no parents living? Yes, a father. Brothers and sisters? One brother, two sisters. Same mother, same father? Yes. But he would not *automatically* share the guinea with them, though he might *choose* to do so.

The woman who'd pulled his arm looked amused at first, then, when she was sure she'd understood, horrified. And so it went on. Because the questions were very carefully chosen, they gradually formed an impression – and not a vague impression either, in some respects quite precise – of the life of a bachelor don in a Cambridge college. Hilarity was the main response. And if the questions had led on to more intimate territory? If he'd been able, or willing, to lay before them the whole constricting business of trying to fit into society, of living under and around and outside the law, what would have been their reaction then? Laughter. They'd have gone on laughing. They would not have known how to pity him. He looked up, at the blue, empty sky, and realized that their view of *his* society was neither more nor less valid than his of theirs. No bearded elderly white man looked down on them, endorsing one set of values and condemning the other. And with that realization, the whole frame of social and moral rules that keeps individuals imprisoned – and sane – collapsed, and for a moment he was in the same position as these drifting, dispossessed people. A condition of absolute free-fall.

Then, next day, after a restless night, he and Hocart transferred to a tramp steamer for the last stage of the journey, and there he met the logical end product of the process of free-fall – the splat on the pavement, as it were – Brennan.

Smells of engine oil and copra, of sweaty human beings sleeping too close together in the little covered cabin on deck. Above their heads, offering no clear reference point to northern eyes, foreign constellations wheeled and turned.

Brennan slept opposite, his profile, under a fringe of greying curls, like that of a Roman emperor's favourite run to seed. He snored, gargled, stopped breathing, gargled again, muttered a protest as if he thought somebody else had woken him, returned to sleep. On the other side of the cabin was Father Michael, trailing behind him the atmosphere of the theological college he'd not long left behind – cups of cocoa and late-night discussions on chastity in other people's bedrooms. Then Hocart, looking much younger than twenty-five, his upper lip pouting on every breath.

Rivers supposed he must have slept eventually, though it seemed no time at all before they were stretching and stumbling out on deck.

The deckhands, emerging from their airless hell-hole next to the engine, swabbed passengers down along with the deck. They finished off with a bucket of cold water thrown full into the face so that one was left gasping and blinded. Brennan stood, eyes closed, one hand resting between his plump breasts, a hirsute Aphrodite, water dripping from his nose, his foreskin, the hairs on his wrinkled and baggy scrotum. It was impossible to dislike somebody who brought such enormous zest to the minute-by-minute business of living.

As the sun rose, beating down on to the steaming deck, they began the day-long search for patches of shade. Father Michael and Hocart came close to quarrelling about the record of missionaries in the islands. Hocart was the product of a Victorian vicarage, and something of a rebel. Michael obviously thought he'd fallen among atheists, or worse. Brennan listened to the argument, scratched his neck, then gathered phlegm in his throat, a rich, bubbling sound – his zest for life became a bit much at times – and spat it on the deck, where he inspected it carefully, and Rivers, cursing his medical training, found himself inspecting it too. 'I knew a missionary once,' Brennan said, with a look of placid, lazy malice. 'Didn't speak a word of the language – just sets up shop – Jesus saves. And then he starts to get worried 'cause they all come flocking round but he can't get the buggers to kneel down. So down on his knees he goes. "What's the word for this?" Well *you* know and *I* know,' Brennan said, turning to Rivers, 'there's only one thing *they* do kneeling down. Come next Sunday, bloody great congregation, up he stands – raises his arms.' He looked at Michael and, in an amazingly pure counter-tenor, sang, 'Let us fuck.'

A bray of laughter from the open door of the engine-room where the skipper stood, wiping his fingers on an oily rag.

'I wish you'd leave Michael alone,' Rivers said to Hocart after the others had gone below deck.

'Why? He's an arrogant little –'

'He's a baby.'

But Hocart, a baby himself, saw no need for mercy.

After dark, packed round the rickety table on which they ate their dinner, there was no escaping each other's company. Elbows jarred, knees joggled, the leather seats tormented patches of prickly heat. Much covert and not so covert scratching of backsides went on. The skipper joined them for the meal, but contributed little to the conversation, preferring to be amused in silence. His trade had made him a connoisseur of social discomfort.

Brennan, sensing that Rivers liked him, embarked on what threatened to become his life story, interspersed with swigs of whisky and great breathy revelations of dental decay. He showed Rivers a photograph of his three naked brown babies tumbling over each other in the dust. Behind them, face, neck and breasts covered in tattoos, stood a young girl. 'She must be from Lepers Island,' Rivers said.

Brennan took the photograph back and stared at it. 'Yeh, that's right. *Bitch*.'

He seemed about to say more. Rivers said quickly, 'I didn't realize you'd been in the New Hebrides.'

'Started there.'

He'd started as a 'blackbirder', as so many of the older traders had, kidnapping natives to work on the Queensland plantations, and he was frank about his methods too. Make friends with them, invite them on board ship, get them drunk and Bob's your Uncle. By the time they come round they're out at sea and there's bugger all they can do about it. Used to give the girls a bit of a run round the deck, mind. We-ll why not, they're all gunna get their arses fucked off when they get to the plantations anyway. 'Do you know,' he went on, leaning across the table in search of somebody to shock, and fixing on Michael, though Hocart's expression might have made him the more obvious choice, 'you can buy a woman – *white*, mind – for forty quid in Sydney?'

'I'd've thought forty quid was a bit steep,' Hocart said.

'*Buy*, man, I'm not talking about fucking rent.'

'So why didn't you?'

'Nah,' Brennan said morosely, swishing whisky round his glass. 'Years on their backs.' He turned to

Rivers. 'Half way through the honeymoon you'd be pissing hedgehogs backwards. *He* knows what I mean,' he said, jerking his thumb at Rivers.

'We all know what you mean,' Hocart said.

The skipper leant forward, smiling a positively old-maidish smile. 'How about a nice game of cards?'

And then there was no further talk, only the creaking of the spirit-lamp above their heads, and the plump slap of cards on the table. Rivers, amused, watched Hocart slowly realize that when confronted by a dwindling stock of coins, Father Michael cheated and Brennan didn't.

Next morning – a small triumph for Melanesia – Father Michael, who'd hitherto crouched over a bucket to wash, stripped off with the rest of them, his white arum lily of a body with its improbable stamen looking almost shocking beside Brennan's.

The conversation that morning meandered on amicably enough, as they leaned together, sweating, in their patches of shade, until a smudge of blue-green on the horizon restored them to separateness.

By late afternoon they'd moored by a rotting landing stage on Eddystone, and clambered ashore to supervise the unloading of their stores. Rivers was used to missionized islands where canoes paddled out to meet the incoming steamer, brown faces, white eyes, flashing smiles, while others gathered at the landing stage, ready to carry bags up to the mission station for a few sticks of tobacco or even sheer

Christian goodwill. A cheerful picture, as long as you didn't notice the rows and rows of crosses in the mission graveyard, men and women in the prime of life dead of the diseases of the English nursery: whooping cough, measles, diphtheria, chicken pox, scarlet fever – all were fatal here. And the mission boat carried them from island to island, station to station, remorselessly, year after year.

Instead of that – nothing. Nobody appeared. Rivers and Hocart waved till the steamer dwindled to a point on the glittering water, then lugged the tent and enough food for the night up to a small clearing a hundred yards or so above the beach. Spread out below them was the Bay of Narovo. The village, whose huts they could just see between the trees, was also called Narovo.

'Aren't we a bit close?' Hocart asked.

'We don't want to be *too* far away. If we're isolated we'll be frightening. The wicked witch lives in the *wood*, remember.'

'What do you suppose they'll do?'

Rivers shrugged. 'They'll be along.'

By the time they'd erected the tent the swift tropical darkness was falling. After sunset the island breathed for a moment in silence; from the bush arose the buzz of different insects, the cries of different birds. Rivers was intensely aware of the fragility of the small lighted area round the tent. He kept peering into the trees and thought he saw dark shapes flitting between the trunks, but still nobody appeared.

After a meal of tinned meat and turnipy pineapple, Hocart said he would lie down. He looked utterly exhausted, and Rivers suspected he might be running a slight fever. Shrouded in his mosquito net, Hocart talked for a while, then switched off his torch and turned over to sleep.

Rivers sat at a table immediately outside the tent, trying to mend the oil-lamp which was smoking badly. A small figure alone in the clearing, in a storm of pale wings, for every moth in the bush appeared and fluttered round the light. Now and then one succeeded in finding a way in, and there was a quick sizzle, a flare, more smoke. Rivers shook out the charred corpse and started again. An oddly nerve-racking business, this. Working so close to the light, he was almost blinded and could see virtually nothing even when he raised his head. He was aware of the thick darkness of the bush around him, but more as a pressure on his mind than through his senses. Once he stopped, thinking he heard a flute being played in the village. He sniffed the oil on his fingers, wiped his chin on the back of his hand, and sat back for a rest, his retinas aching as they do after an optician has shone his torch on to them. He took his glasses off and wiped them on his shirt. When he put them on again he saw a figure had come out from among the trees, and was standing on the edge of the clearing. A man in early middle age, white lime streaks in his hair, around the eye sockets, and along the cheek and jaw-bones, so that it seemed —

until he caught the glint of eye white – that he was looking at a skull. He sat absolutely still, as the man came towards him. Alone, or apparently alone. He indicated the other chair, thinking it might be refused, but his visitor sat down, inclined his head slightly, and smiled.

Rivers pointed to himself and said his name.

A thin brown hand raised to his shell necklace. 'Njiru.'

They stared at each other. Rivers thought he ought to offer food, but the only food easily available was the remains of the pineapple, and he was chary of breaking off the encounter by going into the tent to look for it.

Njiru was deformed. Without the curvature of the spine he would have been a tall man – by Melanesian standards very tall – and he carried himself with obvious authority. In addition to the shell necklace he wore ear-rings, arm rings and bracelets all made of shells, and somehow it was immediately apparent that these ornaments had great value. His earlobes, elongated by the constant wearing of heavy shells, almost brushed his shoulders when he moved. The eyes were remarkable: hooded, piercing, intelligent, shrewd. Wary.

They went on staring at each other, reluctant to start exploring their shared resource of pidgin, aware, perhaps, even in these first moments, of how defective an instrument it would be for what they needed to say to each other.

Suddenly Njiru pointed to the lamp. 'Baggerup.'

Rivers was so surprised he laughed out loud. '*No*, No baggerup. I mend.'

Njiru was the eldest son of Rembo, the chief who controlled the most important cults on the island. Because of his deformity, he'd never been able to compete with other young men, in canoeing, fishing, building or war. By way of compensation, he'd devoted himself to thought and learning, and, in particular, to the art of healing. His abilities would have made him remarkable in any society. On Eddystone, his power rested primarily on the number of spirits he controlled. The people made no distinction between knowledge and power, either in their own language or in pidgin. 'Njiru knows Mateana' meant Njiru had the power to cure the diseases caused by Mateana. Similarly, Rivers was told within a few days of arriving on the island that Njiru 'knew' Ave. Without in the least understanding the significance of what he'd been told, he repeated it to Njiru. 'Kundaite he say you know Ave.'

A snort of derision. 'Kundaite he speak *gammon*.'

He was by far the best interpreter and – when he chose – the most reliable informant, capable of making rigorous distinctions between what he knew and what he merely supposed, between evidence and hypothesis. But he did not generally choose to share information. If knowledge was power, then Njiru kept a firm grasp on his. Indeed, at first he would do no more than translate passively what others said. In particular, he acted as interpreter between Rivers and Rinambesi.

Rinambesi was the oldest man on the island, the liveliest, and, after Njiru, the most vigorous. He seemed immune to the apathy and depression that many of the younger islanders seemed to feel, perhaps because he lived so much in the glories of the past. Like very old people the world over, he was hazy about yesterday's events, but vividly remembered the triumphs of his youth. He'd been a great head-hunter once, ferocious enough to have secured the rare privilege of a second wife. His memory for the genealogies of the islanders was phenomenal, and this was chiefly what brought Rivers to him. And yet, time and time again, the flow of information faltered, though it was not immediately obvious why.

Sexual intercourse between unmarried young people was very free, though 'free' was perhaps the wrong word, since every act had to be preceded by a payment of shells by the young man to the girl's parents. After marriage complete fidelity was required, and one expression of this was that one must never utter the name of an ex-lover.

All the women's names in Rinambesi's generation had to be left blank. Looking at the row of cards in front of him, Rivers turned to Njiru. 'This fellow make fuck-fuck *all* women?'

A gleam of amusement. 'Yes.'

Rivers threw the pencil down. Rinambesi, grinning toothlessly, was making a deeply unsuccessful attempt to look modest. Rivers started to laugh and after a moment Njiru joined in, a curious moment of kinship across the gulf of culture.

A thread-like wail from the baby Njiru held in his hands, one palm cradling the head, the other the buttocks, a morsel of black-eyed misery squirming in between.

Her name was Kwini and her mother was dead. Worse than that, she'd died in childbirth, which made her an evil spirit, likely to attempt to reclaim her child. The body had been dumped at sea, a bundle of rags strapped between the breasts to fool the mother into thinking she had her baby with her, but still . . . Kwini's failure to thrive was attributed to her mother's attempts to get her back.

She certainly *wasn't* thriving: skin hung in loose folds from her thighs. Rivers looked round the circle at her grandmother's wrinkled dugs, the flat chest of her nine-year-old sister, the highly developed pectoral muscles of her father. He asked what she was being fed on. Mashed-up yams softened by spit was the answer. The tiny hands clawed the air as if she would wring life out of it.

Njiru passed the leaves he was holding several times between his legs and then, stretching to his full height, attached them to the rafters at the gable end, where the scare ghost shivered in the draught. 'Come down and depart, you ghost, her mother; do not haunt this child and let her live.'

'*Will* she live?' Rivers asked.

He had his own opinion, but wanted to know what Njiru would say. Njiru spread his hands.

On their way back to Narovo, Rivers questioned him about the ghosts of women who died in childbirth. This was not a rare form of death, since the custom was for women to give birth alone, and there was no tradition of midwifery. Such ghosts could not be named, he already knew that. In the genealogies they were referred to as evil spirits. It had startled him at first to be told quite casually that such and such a man had married 'an evil spirit'.

They were called *tomate pa na savo* – the ghosts of the confining house – Njiru explained, and they were dreaded, since their chief aim was to ensure that as many other women as possible should die in the same way.

One ghost in particular inspired dread: Ange Mate. She was more powerful, more vengeful than any other ghost of the confining house. Rivers had been taken to see Ange Mate's well, a hole in the ground which had once been a living spring, now choked with coconut husks. Still, he sensed there was something more that Njiru was reluctant to tell him. 'What does she *do*?' he wanted to know. It puzzled him that the men were obviously frightened of her, if it were true that the *tomate pa na savo* selected women as their victims.

Reluctantly, Njiru said she lay in wait for men, particularly for men who fell asleep on the beach at Pa Njale. 'But what does she do?' A ripple of amusement among Njiru's retinue, a strange response in view of the obvious terror she inspired. Then he guessed. When Ange Mate came upon a man sleeping she forced him to have sex with her. 'Is he goodfellow after?' Rivers asked.

No, seemed to be the answer, he suffered from a long list of complaints, not the least of which was a disappearing penis. Rivers would have liked to ask about the psychological effects, but that was almost impossible. The language of introspection was simply not available.

By the time they reached Narovo, the sun was low in the sky. Rivers went down to the beach, following the narrow bush path that petered out into fine white sand. Hocart's head was a dark sleek ball, far out, but then he saw Rivers, waved and shouted.

Slowly Rivers waded out, looking down, rather liking the dislocation the refraction of the light produced, the misalignment of knees and feet. As usual he was joined by a shoal of little darting black fish who piloted him out into deeper waters – always a moment of absolute magic. Behind him, the bluish shadows of rocks crept over the white sand.

After their swim they lay in the shallows, talking over the events of the day. In the rough division of labour they'd mapped out between them, death, funerary rites and skull houses belonged to Hocart, ghosts, sex, marriage and kinship to Rivers, but it had already become clear that no division really made sense. Each of them was constantly acquiring information relating to one of the other's specialities.

Hocart, though, was in a mood to tease. 'Why've I got death when you've got sex?' he wanted to know. 'Ghosts and sex don't go together. Now ghosts and *death* . . .'

'All right, you can have ghosts.'

'*No* . . .' Hocart began, and then laughed.

Not true anyway, Rivers thought. On Eddystone ghosts and sex *did* go together, or so at least it must seem to men who fell asleep on the beach at Pa Njale and woke between the ravening thighs of Ange Mate.

They lay in silence, almost too lazy to speak, as the shadows lengthened and the sun began its precipitate descent. Nightfall on Eddystone was abrupt, as if some positive force of darkness in the waters of the bay had risen up and swallowed the sun. At last, driven back to shore by the cooling water, they snatched up their clothes and ran, laughing, back to the tent.

Mbuko was dying of a disease caused by the spirits of Kita, and had no more than a few hours to live.

Kita, Njiru explained, causes a man to waste away 'till he too small all bone he got no meat'. Certainly Mbuko could not have been more emaciated. He looked more like an anatomical drawing than a man, except for the persistent flutter of his heart under the stretched skin. He lay on the raised wooden platform that was used for sleeping, though nobody else now slept in the hut. Njiru said they were afraid. Outside, bright sunshine, people coming and going. Now and then a neighbour would look in to see if he were still alive. 'Soon,' the people sitting round would say, indifferently, shaking their heads. Some were obviously amused or repelled by his plight. '*Rakiana*' was the word one heard over and over again. *Rakiana*. Thin.

Even Njiru who, within the framework of his culture, was a compassionate man (and we can none of us claim more, Rivers thought), seemed to feel, not indifference or contempt exactly, but that Mbuko had become merely a problem to be solved. Njiru looked across the barely breathing heap of bones at Rivers and said, '*Mate*.'

'*Mate*' in all the dictionaries was translated as 'dead'.

'No *mate*,' Rivers said, breathing deeply and pointing to Mbuko's chest.

There and then, across the dying man, he received a tutorial, not unlike those he remembered from his student days in Bart's. *Mate* did not mean dead, it designated a state of which death was the appropriate outcome. Mbuko was *mate* because he was critically ill. Rinambesi, though quite disgustingly healthy, still with a keen eye for the girls, was also *mate* because he'd lived to an age when if he wasn't dead he damn well ought to be. The term for actual death, the moment when the *sagena* – here Njiru breathed in, slapping his belly in the region of the diaphragm – the 'something he stop long belly' departed, was *mate ndapu*. In pidgin, 'die finish'. 'Was the *sagena* the same as the soul?' Rivers wanted to know. 'Of course it wasn't,' Njiru snapped, nostrils flaring with impatience. Oh God, it was Bart's all over again. *Heaven help the unsuspecting public when we let you loose on them.* The problem with Mbuko, Njiru pressed on, as with all those who fell into the power of Kita, was that he couldn't die. He seemed to be making a very creditable stab at it, Rivers thought rebelliously. Kita could 'make him small', but not kill him. '*Kita pausia,*' Njiru said, stroking Mbuko. 'Kita loves him?' Rivers suggested. No, Njiru would know the word. Kita was nursing him.

Njiru hung malanjari leaves from the gable end of the hut where the scare ghost shivered in the draught, and began chanting the prayer of exorcism. His shadow came and went across the dying man's face. At one point Rivers got cramp in his legs and tried to stand up, but the people on either side of him pulled him down. He must not walk under the malanjari leaves, they said, or he would waste away and become like Mbuko.

Hocart came into the hut, edging round the walls, keeping well clear of the malanjari leaves, until he reached Rivers. Now that all eyes were focused on

Njiru, Rivers could take Mbuko's pulse. He shook his head. 'Not long.'

Scattered all round were bits of calico and bark cloth streaked with mucus, with here and there a great splash of red where Mbuko had haemorrhaged. Now gobs of phlegm rose into his mouth and he lacked the strength even to spit them out. Rivers found a fresh piece of cloth, moistened it with his own saliva, and cleaned the dying man's mouth. His tongue came out and flicked across his dry lips. Then a rattle in the throat, a lift and flare of the rib-cage, and it was over. One of the women wailed briefly, but the wail faltered into silence, and she put a hand over her mouth as if embarrassed.

Rivers automatically reached out to close the eyes, then stopped himself. Mbuko's body was bound into a sitting position by bands of calico passed round his neck and under his knees. He was tied to a pole, and two men carried him out into the open air. Rivers and Hocart followed the little group down the path to the beach.

The body was propped up, still in a sitting position, in the stern of a canoe, his shield and axe were placed beside him, and he was quickly paddled out to sea. Rivers waited until the canoe was a shadow on the glittering waters of the bay, then went back to the hut and gathered together the stained cloths, which he buried at a safe distance from the village. As he scraped dry earth over the heap of rags, he felt an intense craving to scrub his arms up to the elbow in boiled water. That would have to wait till he got back to the tent. For the moment he contented himself with wiping his palms several times hard on the seat of his trousers.

He went back to the beach, where a disgruntled Hocart lingered by the waterline. They had both been hoping that this death would shed light on the cult of the skull. Instead . . .

'They don't keep the skull,' Hocart said.

As they watched, the paddlers in the canoe tipped the corpse unceremoniously over the side, where it sank beneath the water with scarcely a splash.

Rivers shook his head. 'I'm afraid what we need is a proper death.'

NINE

Wyatt had embarked on some interminable anecdote about a brothel he'd been to in which there was a whore so grotesquely fat you got your money back if you succeeded in fucking her.

Prior rested his cheek on the cold glass of the train window, glancing sidelong at the doubled reflection of cheekbone and eye, and then deeper into the shadowy compartment with its transparent occupants laughing and gesturing, floating shapes on the rain-flawed pane.

A roar of laughter as the story climaxed. Gregg, happily married with a small daughter, smiled tolerantly. Hallet uneasily joined in. One young lad brayed so loudly his virginity became painfully apparent to everybody but himself. Only Owen made no attempt to disguise his disgust, but then he hated 'the commercials', as he called them.

They'd been on the train for three hours, jammed together on slatted wooden seats, stale sweat in armpits, groin and feet, a smoky smell of urine where some half-baked idiot had pissed into the wind.

Five minutes later the train slipped into the dark station, a few discreet naphtha flares the only light.

Prior walked along to the trucks, where the men were stirring. Strange faces peered blearily up at him as he swept the torch across them, shading the beam in his cupped hand, so that he saw them – not figuratively but quite literally – in a glow of blood. They were not his, or anybody's, men, just an anonymous draft that he'd shepherded a stage further to their destination.

This section of the train had stopped well short of the platform, and there was a big drop from the truck. Repeated crunches of gravel under boots as men, still dazed from sleep, grappled with the shock of rain and windswept darkness. Marshalled together, they half stumbled, half marched alongside the train, on to the platform and through into the station yard where, after an interminable wait, guides finally appeared, their wet capes reflecting a fish gleam at the sky, as they gesticulated and gabbled, directing units to their billets.

Prior saw his draft settled in a church hall, said goodbye and wished them luck. Their faces turned towards him registered nothing, subdued to the impersonality of the process that had them in its grip.

Then he was free. Felt it too, following the guide through unlit streets, past that sandbagged witch's tit of a cathedral, along the canal accompanied in the water by a doddering old crone of a moon.

The night, the silent guide, the effort of not slipping on broken pavements, sharpened his senses. An overhanging branch of laburnum flung a scattering of cold raindrops into his eyes and he was startled by the intensity of his joy. A joy perhaps not unconnected with the ruinous appearance of these houses. Solid bourgeois houses they must have been in peacetime, the homes of men making their way in the world, men who'd been sure that certain things would never change, and where were they now? Every house in the road was damaged, some ruined. The ruins stood out starkly, black jagged edges in the white gulf of moonlight.

'Here you are, sir.'

A gate hanging from its hinges, roses massed round a broken pergola, white ruffled blooms with a heavy scent, unpruned, twisting round each other for support. Beyond, paths and terraces overgrown with weeds. Lace curtains hanging limp behind cracked or shattered glass; on the first floor the one window still unbroken briefly held the moon.

The guide preceded him up the path. No lock on the door, black and white tiles in the hall – a sudden sharp memory of Craiglockhart – and then a glimmer of light at the top of the stairs and Hallet appeared, holding a candle. 'Come on up. Mind that stair.'

Hallet had got his sleeping-bag out and arranged his belongings carefully in a corner of what must once have been the master bedroom. His fiancée's photograph stood on a chair.

'Potts and Owen are upstairs.'

Prior went to the window and looked out at the houses opposite, fingering the lace curtains that were stiff with dried rain and dirt. 'This is all right, isn't it?' he said suddenly, turning into the room.

They grinned at each other.

'Bathroom's just opposite,' Hallet said, pointing it out like a careful host.

'You mean it works?'

'Well, the bucket works.'

Prior sat down abruptly on the floor and yawned. He was too tired to care where he was. They lit cigarettes and shared a bar of chocolate, Prior leaning against the wall, Hallet sitting cross-legged on his sleeping-bag, both of them staring round like big-eyed children, struggling to take in the strangeness.

It'll wear off, Prior thought, lighting a candle and venturing across the landing to find a room of his own. It'll all seem normal in the morning.

But it didn't. Prior woke early, and lay lazily watching the shadows of leaves on a wall that the rising sun had turned from white to gold. He was just turning over to go back to sleep, when something black flickered across the room. He waited, and saw a swallow lift and loop through the open window and out into the dazzling air.

On that first morning he looked out on to a green jungle of garden, sun-baked, humming with insects, the once formal flower-beds transformed into brambly tunnels in which hidden life rustled and burrowed. He rested his arms on the window-sill and peered out, cautiously, through the jagged edges of glass, at Owen and Potts, who were carrying a table from one of the houses across the road. He shouted down to them, as they paused for breath, and they waved back.

He would have said that the war could not surprise him, that somewhere on the Somme he had mislaid the capacity to be surprised, but the next few days were a constant succession of surprises.

They had nothing to do. They were responsible for no one. The war had forgotten them.

There were only two items of furniture that went with the house. One was a vast carved oak sideboard that must surely have been built in the dining-room, for it could never have been brought in through the door; the other was a child's painted rocking-horse on the top floor of the house, in a room with bars at the window. Everything else they found for themselves. Prior moved in and out of the ruined houses, taking whatever caught his eye, and the houses, cool and dark in the midday heat, received him placidly. He brought his trophies home and arranged them carefully in his room, or in the dining-room they all shared.

In the evenings he and Hallet, Owen and Potts lit candles, sitting around the table that was Owen's chief find, and with the tall windows, the elaborately moulded ceilings, the bowls of roses and the wine created a fragile civilization, a fellowship on the brink of disaster.

And then ruined it by arguing about the war. Or Potts and Hallet argued. Potts had been a science student at Manchester University, bright, articulate, cynical in the thorough-going way of those who have not so far encountered much to be cynical about. The war, he insisted loudly, flushed with wine, was feathering the nests of profiteers. It was being fought to safeguard access to the oil-wells of Mesopotamia. It had nothing, absolutely *nothing*, to do with Belgian neutrality, the rights of small nations or anything like that. And if Hallet thought it had, then Hallet was a naïve idiot. Hallet came from an old army family and had been well and expensively educated to think as little as possible; confronted by Potts, he floundered, but then quickly began to formulate beliefs that he had hitherto assumed everybody shared.

Prior and Owen exchanged secretive smiles, though neither probably could have said of what the secret consisted. Owen was playing with the fallen petals of roses he'd picked that afternoon. Pink, yellow, white roses, but no red roses, Prior saw.

'What do *you* think?' Potts asked, irritated by Prior's silence.

'What do I think? I think what you're saying is basically a conspiracy theory, and like all conspiracy theories it's optimistic. What you're saying is, OK the war isn't being fought for the reasons we're told, but it *is* being fought for a reason. It's not benefiting the people it's supposed to be benefiting, but it *is* benefiting somebody. And I don't believe that, you see. I think things are actually much worse than you think because there isn't any kind of rational justification left. It's become a self-perpetuating system. Nobody benefits. Nobody's in control. Nobody knows how to stop.'

Hallet looked from one to the other. 'Look, all this just isn't *true*. You're – no, not you – *people* are letting themselves get demoralized because they're having to pay a higher price than they thought they were going to have to pay. But it doesn't alter the basic facts. We *are* fighting for the legitimate interests of our own country. We *are* fighting in defence of Belgian neutrality. We *are* fighting for French independence. *We* aren't in Germany. They *are* in France.' He looked round the table and, like a little boy, said pleadingly, 'This is still a just war.'

'You say we kill the Beast,' Owen said slowly. 'I say we fight because men lost their bearings in the night.' He smiled at their expressions, and stood up. 'Shall we open another bottle?'

Alone that night, the smell of snuffed-out candle lingering on the air, Prior remembered the bowl of pink and gold and white roses, but did not bother to recall Potts's and Hallet's arguments. This house they shared was so strange in terms of what the war had hitherto meant that he wanted to fix the particular sights and sounds and smells in his mind. He felt

enchanted, cocooned from anything that could possibly cause pain, though even as the thought formed, a
trickle of plaster leaked from the ceiling of the back
bedroom where a shell had struck, the house bleeding
quietly from its unstaunchable wound.

In the mornings he went into town, wandering
round the stalls that had been set up in front of the
cathedral to sell 'souvenirs'. So many souvenirs were
to be found in the rubble of the bombed city that
trade was not brisk. Prior saw nothing that he wanted
to buy, and anyway he had a shelf of souvenirs at
home, mainly collected on his first time in France.
He'd thought of them often at Craiglockhart as
Rivers probed his mind for buried memories of his
last few weeks in France. Souvenirs, my God. When
the mind will happily wipe itself clean in the effort
to forget.

On the way home he saw Owen and Potts ahead
of him, and hurried to catch them up. Owen had
found a child's lace-trimmed surplice in the rubble
near the cathedral and wore it as a scarf, the cloth
startlingly white against his sunburnt neck. Potts
hugged a toby-jug to his chest, stoutly refusing to
admit it was hideous. They turned off the road and
cut through the back gardens, entering a world that
nobody would have guessed at, from the comparative
normality of the road.

A labyrinth of green pathways led from garden to
garden, and they slipped from one to another, over

broken walls or through splintered fences, skirting bramble-filled craters, brushing down paths overgrown with weeds, with flowers that had seeded themselves and become rank, with overgrown roses that snagged their sleeves and pulled them back. Snails crunched under their boots, nettles stung their hands, cuckoo spit flecked a bare neck, but the secret path wound on. Hundreds of men, billeted as they were in these ruined houses, had broken down every wall, every fence, forced a passage through all the hedges, so that they could slip unimpeded from one patch of ground to the next. The war, fought and refought over strips of muddy earth, paradoxically gave them the freedom of animals to pass from territory to territory, unobserved. And something of an animal's alertness too, for just as Owen pushed aside an elderberry branch at the entrance to their own garden, his ears caught a slight sound, and he held up his hand.

Hallet was in the garden, undressing. Dappled light played across his body, lending it the illusion of fragility, the greenish tinge of ill-health, though he was as hard and sun-tanned as the rest of them. As they watched, not calling out a greeting as by now they should have done, he stepped out of his drawers and out of time, standing by the pool edge, thin, pale, his body where the uniform had hidden it starkly white. Sharp collar-bones, bluish shadows underneath. He was going to lie down in the overgrown goldfish pool with its white lilies and golden insects fumbling the pale flowers. His toes curled round the mossy edge as he gingerly lowered himself, gasping as the water hit his balls.

They strolled across the tall grass towards him and stood looking down. Legs bloated-looking under water, silver bubbles trapped in his hair, cock slumped on his thigh like a seal hauled out on to the rocks. He looked up at them lazily, fingers straying through his bush, freeing the bubbles.

'Enjoying yourself?' Prior asked, nodding at the hand.

Hallet laughed, shielding his eyes with his other hand, but didn't move.

'I'd be careful if I were you,' Owen said, in a tight voice. 'I expect those fish are ravenous.'

And not just the fish, Prior thought.

'Anybody want some wine?' Potts asked, going into the house.

They drank it on the terrace, Hallet lying in the pond, till it grew too cold.

'You know they might leave us here,' Owen said, squinting up into the sun.

'Shut up!' Potts said.

Everybody touched wood, crossed fingers, groped for lucky charms: all the small, protective devices of men who have no control over their own fate. No use, Prior thought. Somewhere, outside the range of human hearing, and yet heard by all of them, a clock had begun to tick.

11 September 1918

I don't think it helps Owen that I'm here. And it certainly doesn't help *me* that he's here. We're both walking a tightrope and the last thing either of us wants or needs is to be watched by somebody who knows the full terror of the fall.

At Craiglockhart we avoided each other. It was easy to do that there, in spite of the overcrowding. The labyrinth of corridors, so many turnings, so many alternative routes, you need never meet anybody you didn't want to meet except, now and then, in Rivers's room or Brock's, yourself.

Two incidents this week. We were all in town together and we saw wounded being rushed through the streets – some of them quite bad. Hallet and Potts stared at them, and you could see them thinking, That could be me, in a few days or weeks. Looking at the bandages, trying to imagine what was underneath. Trying not to imagine. Fear: rational, proportionate, *appropriate* fear. And I glanced at Owen and he was indifferent. As I was. I don't mean unsympathetic, *necessarily*. (Though it's amazing what you leave behind when the pack's heavy.)

The other was at supper last night. Hallet was cockahoop because he'd found some flypaper on one of those stalls in the cathedral square. Ever since we arrived we've been plagued by enormous wasps – Owen thinks they're hornets – and by flies, great, buzzing, drunk, heavy, angry, dying bluebottles. And Hallet had solved it all. There was this flypaper buzzing above our heads, revolving first one way, then the other, with its cargo of dead and dying. The sound of summer on the Somme.

I stuck it as long as I could, then climbed up on to the table and took it down, carried it right to the end of the garden and threw it away as far as I could. A pathetic effort – it described a shallow arc and fluttered to the ground. Hallet was quite seriously offended, and of course completely bewildered.

'Don't blame *me* if you all get tummy upsets,' he said.

Owen started to laugh, and I joined in, and neither of us could stop. Hallet and Potts looked from one to the other, grinning like embarrassed dogs. They obviously thought we'd cracked. The trouble is neither of us can be sure they aren't right. When I noticed the absence of red roses, I looked at Owen and saw him noticing that I'd noticed. It's no use.

My servant, Longstaffe

I chose him at bayonet practice. He was running in with blood-curdling yells, stabbing, twisting, withdrawing, running on. I thought, My God, *textbook*. Nothing of the sort – I've realized since that what he was actually doing was *once-moreing* unto the breach at Agincourt.

I had a word with him. He knew why, of course, and he wanted the job. Not a bad life, officer's servant, if you have to be here at all. He told me he'd been a gentleman's gentleman before the war and that clinched it. Later, when we were waiting for the train to Amiens, he owned up. He was an actor. The nearest he'd ever got to being a gentleman's gentleman was playing a butler at the Alhambra, Bradford. A larger part than it sounded, he was anxious to point out, because in this particular production the butler did it – a departure from convention that so little pleased the inhabitants of Bradford that the play had to be taken off after seventeen days.

Perhaps he was sure of me by then. Actually I found all that even more irresistible. Phoney gentleman's gentleman, but then I'm a fairly phoney gentleman myself.

An ironing board of a body, totally flat. Interesting gestures, though. He's the only *man* I've ever known to open doors with his hips. Perfectly plain, nondescript features. No Wanted poster would ever find *him*, but also this curious feeling that his face could be anything he wanted it to be, even beautiful, if the part required it. And burningly ambitious. Knows tracts of Shakespeare off by heart. A curious, old-fashioned romantic patriot, though I don't know why I say that, there's plenty of them about. Hallet, for instance. But then they don't all quote, 'We few, we happy few, we band of brothers,' as he did, quite without embarrassment, the other night while I was getting ready for bed. I said very sourly indeed that a more appropriate quotation for this stage of the war might be: 'I am in blood stepped in so far that should I wade no more . . .' His leap across the room was rather remarkable. He'd slapped a hand across my mouth, and we were staring at each other, dumbstruck, before either of us had time to think, his face chalk-white and I suspect mine as well, each trying to remember what the penalty is for smacking an officer in the gob. Quite possibly death.

Since then we've both gone very quiet, retreating behind the barriers of rank, which are as necessary to his protection as to mine, though not retreating quickly enough. Like the French lines at Agincourt, the barriers have been thoroughly breached.

Friday, the 13th September (No bloody comment)

We're not going to join the battalion. The battalion's coming here to join *us*. I suppose this explains this curious out-of-time holiday we've been having. Ended today, anyway. Rode round inspecting billets.

Weather also changed, which makes the other changes somehow more tolerable. Wind and rain, lowering grey clouds.

Saturday, 14 September

Watched the Manchesters march in, streaming rain, wet capes. Shattered faces, bloodshot eyes. Been having a bad time. One or two faces I recognized *from last year*. Before that? I don't think so. Nobody talks about the losses. What they moaned about, sitting on bales of straw, peeling socks off bloody feet, was the absence of fags. They'd been rolling their own in bits of paper, torn-up envelopes, anything, no tobacco of course, had to smoke weeds they picked by the side of the road and dried by tying them to their packs whenever the sun shone. I've written to Mam and Sarah and everybody else I can think of, begging for Woodbines.

Sunday, 15 September

Joined battalion. Adjutant a nice worried-looking man who suggested I might be battalion Gas Officer (which reveals a sense of humour not otherwise apparent). Marshall-of-the-Ten-Wounds was there, striding up and down, talking loudly. Everything about him – skin, gestures, expression, posture, voice – bold, free, coarse. Unscrupulous? Perhaps, I don't know, at any rate he doesn't care. Enjoys life, I think. By temperament and training a warrior. Bold, cunning, ruthless, resolute, quick of decision, amazingly brave – and if that's a human being then a human being isn't what I am. He's spent his entire adult life gravitating towards fighting – impossible to imagine him leading any other sort of life.

Last night, our last night in Amiens, there was a great storm, flashes of sheet lightning, wind buffeting and slogging the house.

I'd just got to bed when I heard a strange rumbling from above. Hallet appeared in the doorway, white-faced and staring. Only starlight to see by and the whole house with its broken windows so draughty the candle kept being blown out. We got an oil-lamp from the kitchen. Hallet said, 'Is it the guns?' I said, 'Of course it bloody isn't, it's coming from upstairs.'

The stairway leading to the upper floor and the nursery is narrow. We got to the nursery door, paused, looked at each other. Hallet's face illuminated from below had bulges under the eyes like a second lid. I pushed the door open and a blast of cold wind from the broken window hit me. All I saw at first was movement at the far end of the room and then I started to laugh because it was just the rocking-horse rocking. The wind was strong enough to have got it going, I can't think of any other explanation, and its rockers were grinding away on the bare wooden floor.

It ought to have been an anti-climax, and at first I thought it was. We moved the thing away from the window, out of the draught, and went downstairs still laughing, telling Potts, who peered round the door of his room, there was nothing to worry about, go back to sleep, but in my own room with the lamp out I lay awake and all night long that rumbling went on in my head.

TEN

They didn't have to wait long for their proper death.

Ngea was a strong, vigorous man, the most powerful chief on the island after Rembo. Everything to live for, apparently, and yet, as one saw so often in Melanesia, he was not putting up a fight. He lay in his hall, watching the scare ghost turn and turn in the draught, and his life lay, it seemed to Rivers, like a dandelion clock on the palm of his open hand.

His condition was so bad that, at one point, Emele, his wife, and the other women began to wail, the long, drawn out, throbbing, musical wail of the women, but then the sick man rallied slightly and the wailing was abandoned.

Rivers said goodbye to him, promised to see him again tomorrow, though he knew he wouldn't, and walked back to the tent. It was dark by the time he got back, and the green canvas of the tent glowed with the light of the lamp inside it. Hocart's shadow, sharply black and elongated, reached hugely over the roof. Rivers pushed a heavy weight of damp washing aside and went in.

Hocart was sitting cross-legged on the ground, with a pencil held sideways in his mouth, typing up his notes. 'I had to retreat because of the midges.'

'Midges?'

'Whatever.'

Hocart was careless with quinine, careless with the mosquito nets. Rivers threw himself down on his bed, clasped his hands behind his head and watched him. After a few seconds Hocart pulled his shirt over his head, and fanned himself with a sheaf of blank pages. As always the heat of the day was trapped inside the tent, and their bodies ran with sweat.

'You've lost weight,' Rivers said, looking at the shadows between Hocart's ribs. '*Rakiana*, that's the word for you.'

'Well,' Hocart said, round the pencil. 'Just as long as your pal Njiru doesn't start trying to put me out of my misery . . .'

'Is he my pal?'

A quick glance. 'You know he is.'

They worked for a couple of hours, ate some baked yam pudding that Namboko Taru had made for them, worked again, then turned off the lamp.

An hour or so later Rivers heard the sound of footsteps approaching the tent. Hocart had fallen asleep, one raised arm shielding his eyes, the pressure of the pillow pushing his cheek and mouth out of shape. Enough moonlight filtered through the canvas for the shadow of the passer-by to stalk across the inside of the tent. A minute later another, taller shadow followed.

Mali? Mali was a girl of thirteen who'd recently retired to the menstrual hut for the first time. When she'd re-emerged, five days later, arrangements for her defloration were already well in hand. A young man, Runi – he'd be about eighteen – had paid her parents the two arm rings that entitled him to spend twenty consecutive nights with her, and had decided – it was his decision, the girl had no say in the matter – to share the privilege with two of his friends.

Runi was considered a bit of a pest. Only the other day he and his two closest friends – presumably the two he'd invited to share Mali – had climbed some kanarium trees and pelted their unfortunate owners with unripe nuts. Rivers had been reminded of Rag Week. The old people grumbled, and then said, what can you expect, young men cooped up on the island sitting about like old women, instead of being off in their canoes, as they ought to have been, burning villages and taking heads.

Whispers, quite close by. A startled cry, almost a yelp, then grunts, groans, moans, a long crescendo of sobbing cries.

Hocart woke up, listened. 'Oh God, not again.'
'Shush.'

There was a belief on the island that a girl's defloration is never the first time, because her first bleeding means the moon has already lain with her.

The men denied they believed it, insisting it was just a story they told the girls to reassure them, which at least implied a certain tenderness. He hoped so. She looked such a child.

A few minutes' whispering, and the grunts began again. What it is to be eighteen. Another cry, this time definitely male, and footsteps coming back.

'One down, two to go,' Hocart said.

'You realize for the rest of their lives they won't be able to say each other's names?'

No reply. Rivers wondered if he'd drifted back to sleep but when he turned to look, caught the gleam of eye white under the mosquito net. More footsteps. Another shadow climbed the far wall of the tent. A short pause, whispers, then the gasps began again.

Rivers sighed. 'You know, Rinambesi says when a chief dies the last thing that happens, *used* to happen, rather, is a great head-hunting raid, followed by a feast, and all the girls are available *free* to all the warriors. And not reluctant either, apparently. They run into the sea to greet them.'

'Head-hunting as an aphrodisiac?'

'Why not?'

'They seem to be doing all right without it,' Hocart said, as the moans got louder.

'No babies, though.'

The genealogies made grim reading. Families of five or six had been common three or four generations ago. Now many marriages were childless.

The last shadow came and went. Rivers supposed

he must have slept, because it seemed no time at all before the grey early morning light made the mosquito nets as stark and sinister as shrouds. Fowl-he-sing-out was the pidgin term for this pre-dawn hour, and the fowls had started, first a bubbling trickle of notes, always the same bird, he didn't know its name, rising to a frenzy of competing shrieks and cries. But this morning there was a new noise. At first he lay, blinking sleepily, unable to attach meaning to it, but then he realized it was the wailing of women, almost indistinguishable at this distance from the sound of flutes. And he knew Ngea was dead.

They arrived at Ngea's hall to find the corpse bound into the sitting position, propped up against a pillar. A stout stick had been strapped to its back, keeping the head and neck more or less erect – a sort of external spine. Ngea had been bathed and dressed in his best clothes, the lime on his face and in his hair freshly painted, bunches of riria leaves, a plant forbidden to men in life, fastened to his necklaces. Beside him sat his widow, Emele, not crying or wailing with the other women. Very calm, very dignified.

While the women rocked and wailed Njiru was systematically destroying the dead man's possessions, with the exception of the axe which he had set aside. One rare arm ring after another was smashed. Rivers squatted beside Njiru, and asked, in a low voice so as not to disturb the mourners, why they had to be destroyed.

'You make him no good he go Sonto. All same Ngea he stink, he rotten, bymby *he* go Sonto.'

The wailing went on all day, people coming from across the island to bid Ngea farewell. Towards evening – surely, Rivers thought, the disposal of the corpse could not be much longer delayed – Njiru hung a bunch of areca nuts from the rafters by the scare ghost, took down a cluster and held it out in front of them all. He waited till the last wail faltered into silence and every eye was on him, before he began to pray. 'I take down the portion of the chiefly dead.' He bowed towards the corpse, which gazed back at him with glazed eyes. 'Be not angry with us, be not resentful, do not punish us. Let them drink and eat, break coconuts, open the oven. Let the children eat, let the women eat, let the men eat, and be not angry with us, you chiefly dead, oh, oh, oh.'

The curious sound, half howl, half bark, that ended prayers on Eddystone. Njiru put a nut in his mouth and ate it. The people kept glancing nervously at Ngea, but Njiru went round the circle, offering the cluster of nuts to each person in turn. Every man, woman and child took one and ate it. Even a small child had a tiny crunched-up fragment forced into its mouth.

Ngea, without further ceremony, was slung on to a pole and carried off 'into the bush', they said, though in fact they took him to the beach, where he was placed in a stone enclosure – an *era* – with his axe and his shield at his feet. Still propped in a sitting position, his head kept erect by the stick, he looked out over the low stone wall, westwards, to the sunset. Food was left with him, and food for his mother and father, the 'old ghosts'. Once, Njiru said, and there was no mistaking the bitterness in his voice, a slave would have been killed at this moment, and the head placed between Ngea's feet. Njiru glared at Rivers, as if he held him personally responsible for the abolition of the custom. 'Now no all same.'

Next day Rivers went to Ngea's hall to offer his condolences to Emele, and was confronted by an extraordinary sight. A wooden enclosure had been built inside the hall, similar in size and shape to the stone *era* in which Ngea's corpse had been placed, but with higher walls. Inside this enclosure, knees bent up to her chin, hands resting on her feet, in exactly the same position as the corpse of her husband, sat Emele. She had been there, it seemed, all night, and from the expression of agony on her face it was clear cramp had set in.

A number of widows squatted round the enclosure, looking like stumps of wood in their brown bark loincloths. Many of them were his regular informants on such topics as sexual relations, kinship, the arrangement of marriage. Rivers mimicked Emele's cramped position, and asked for the word. *Tongo polo*, they said reluctantly, glancing at each other. *Tongo polo*, he repeated, making sure he'd got the inflection right. But his efforts to speak their language were not received with the usual maternal warmth. He thought they looked nervous.

'How long?' he asked, crouching down again.

But they wouldn't answer, and when he looked round he saw that Njiru had come into the hall and was standing just inside the door.

Before Ngea's death Njiru had agreed to take Rivers and Hocart to see the cave at Pa Na Keru. It was situated near the summit of the highest mountain on the island, and it was a morning's walk, the early stages through thick bush, to get there. Rivers was inclined to think Ngea's death would lead to the postponement of the trip, but when he emerged from the tent the following morning it was to find Njiru, surrounded by a much larger retinue than usual, waiting for him.

He gave them leaves to wear to protect them from the spirits of the mountain, and the whole group set off in good spirits, laughing and chattering, though they fell silent in the late morning as the ground sloped steeply upwards and the muscles of thighs and back began to ache. The path up the mountain, like all the paths on the island, was so narrow that they had to go in single file.

A solemnity had settled over the gathering. Rivers watched the movement of muscles in the back ahead of him, as they toiled and sweated up the slope. Before them was a massive rock-wall with a cave set into it, like a dark mouth. They slipped and slithered up towards it, sending showers of small pebbles peppering down behind them. The final slope was encumbered with big rocks and boulders, and other, flatter stones, some of them sharp. It was near noon, and their shadows had dwindled to ragged black shapes fluttering around their moving feet. One of the men picked up a stone and threw it at the cave mouth to scare away the ghosts. Rivers and Hocart were the only people there never to have visited the cave before, and they were not allowed to approach until Njiru had prayed that they might be protected from disease. While the prayer went on they watched the others bob down and disappear under the hanging wall of rock.

The cave was low but surprisingly deep, deep enough for the far end to be hidden in shadow. A flat stone near the entrance was called the ghost seat. This was where the new ghost sat and occasionally, to pass the time, drew on the walls. Further in, on the cusp of darkness, was another boulder where the old ghosts sat. 'All old *tomate* come and look new *tomate*,' they were told.

Rivers turned to Njiru and pointed to the seat of the old ghosts. 'Man he stink, he rotten, bymby he go Sonto. Why him no go Sonto?' he asked.

Njiru spread his hands.

Various marks on the wall were interpreted as being the drawings of the new ghosts. Hocart started sketching the marks and recording the identifications he was given. A man, a spirit, pigs, a war canoe.

Njiru wanted to pursue the matter of the old ghosts. He did not himself believe, he said, that there were ghosts in the cave. It was a, a . . . His patience with pidgin ran out. A *varavara*, he concluded. As nearly as Rivers could make out, this meant a metaphor, a figure of speech. Increasingly now, when they were alone, they tried to understand concepts in the other's language, to escape from the fogged communication of pidgin. The language barrier was more formidable than Rivers had initially supposed, for in addition to the ordinary dialect there was the 'high speech' of ritual, myth and prayer. There was also, though he had not been permitted to hear it, *talk blong tomate*: the language of ghosts.

While talking, they had unconsciously wandered deeper into the cave. Now Rivers touched Njiru's arm and pointed to a narrow slit in the back wall. They had to clamber over fallen rocks to reach it, and when they did, it seemed to be too small to admit even a very thin man. Once, Njiru said, the cave had been 'good fellow' right into the centre of the mountain, but then an earthquake had dislodged part of the roof. Rivers knelt down and peered into the darkness. If he crawled he was sure he could get through. And he'd brought a torch with him, not knowing whether the cave would be dark or not. He turned on his back and wriggled through, catching his arm, feeling a wetness that he thought might be blood. On the other side he stood up tentatively, and then stretched his arms high above his head. He had a sense of immense space around him. The cave was big. He was reaching in his back pocket for the torch when he realized Njiru was following him through. He put his hand into the hole, trying to shield the other man's deformed back from the jagged edge of the rock.

They stood together, breathing. Rivers shone his torch at the floor and cautiously they moved deeper into the cave. He put a hand out and touched something that slithered away under his fingers, then swung the torch round, a weak sickly ring of yellow light that revealed what for a second made him doubt his sanity: the walls were alive. They were covered in heaving black fur.

Bats, of course. After the first jolt of fear, it was obvious. He directed the torch at the ceiling where more bats hung, thousands of them, hundreds of thousands perhaps, little sooty stalactites. As the torch swept over them, they raised their heads, frenzied little faces, wet pink gums, white fangs, all jabbering with fear.

Moving very slowly and quietly, not wanting to disturb them further, he again shone the torch at the ground, so that they stood, disconnected feet and legs, in a pool of light. He shouldn't have been startled by the bats, because he knew – Njiru had mentioned it – that in the old days it had been a regular outing for the men of Narovo to go and hunt bats in the cave at Pa Na Keru. But then one day, or so the legend said, a man took the wrong turning and, while his companions wound their way *out* of the mountain, his every step was leading him deeper into it. At last he stumbled upon another exit, and made his way back to the village, but, though he'd been missing less than a week, he returned an old man. He stayed with his mother for three days, but then his face turned black and he crumbled away into dust.

Nobody had followed them into the inner cave. Hocart was busy with his drawings and the islanders were presumably afraid of the legend. Was Njiru also afraid? If he was, he didn't show it. They could hear talk and laughter only a few feet away, in the outer cave, but their isolation in this hot, fur-lined darkness was complete.

This was the first time he'd been alone with Njiru since Ngea's death, and Rivers wanted to talk about Emele: partly because any ceremony connected with the death of a chief was important, but partly too because he felt concern for the woman herself.

'*Tongo polo,*' he said.

He felt Njiru withdraw.

'How long?' he persisted. 'How many days?'

Njiru shook his head. 'Man old time he savvy *tongo polo*, now no all same.'

The last words were accompanied by a dismissive chopping movement of his hand, not intended to make contact with anything, but his fingers clipped the end of the torch and sent it clattering to the ground, where it continued to shine, a single yellow eye focused on them in the darkness. Then the walls lifted off and came towards them. Rivers barely had time to see the beam of light become a tunnel filled with struggling shapes before he was enclosed in flapping squeaking screaming darkness, blinded, his skin shrinking from the contact that never came.

He stood with eyes closed, teeth clenched, senses so inundated they'd virtually ceased to exist, his mind shrunk to a single point of light. Keep still, he told himself, they won't touch you. And after that he didn't think at all but endured, a pillar of flesh that the soles of his feet connected to the earth, the bones of his skull vibrating to the bats' unvarying high-pitched scream.

The cave mouth disgorged fleeing human beings; behind them the bats streamed out in a dark cloud that furled over on to itself as it rose, like blood flowing from a wound under water. Eventually, shocked into silence, they all turned to stare, and watched for a full minute, before the stream thinned to a trickle.

Inside the cave, Rivers and Njiru opened their eyes. Rivers was not aware of having moved during the exodus, indeed would have sworn that he had not, but he discovered that he was gripping Njiru's hand. He felt . . . not dazed, dazed was the wrong word. The opposite of dazed. Almost as if a rind had been pared off, naked, unshelled, lying in contact with the earth. Wonderingly, in the intense silence, they gazed round the grey granite walls, with here and there in the vastness black squares of baby bats hung upside-down to await their mothers' return.

A shaft of sunlight struck his eyes.

'Sorry,' Miss Irving said, and pulled the curtain a little way back. 'What sort of night did you have?

'So-so.'

He seemed to have spent the entire night between hot, fur-lined walls and the fur had got on to his teeth.

'Here's your tea,' she said, putting the tray across his knees.

He drank it gratefully, sending out messages to various parts of his body to find out what the situation was. Ghastly, seemed to be the general response.

'Don't you think you should have a doctor?' She smiled at him. 'Doctor.'

'No. All he'd do is tell me to stay in bed and drink plenty of fluids. I can tell myself that.'

'All right. Ring if there's anything you want.'

'Would you mind drawing the curtains?'

The darkness reminded him of the cave. All night he'd had bats clinging to the inside walls of his skull. But now at least there was a breeze, the curtains breathed gently. But he was still too hot. He kicked off the covers, unbuttoned his jacket and flapped the edges, ran his tongue round his cracked lips. Hot.

★

The sun beat down the moment they left the cave. It was past noon, but the hard bright white rocks reflected heat into their faces. They walked more slowly on the way back, Rivers intensely aware of Njiru walking just ahead of him, though they did not speak. Near the village they began, by mutual consent, to lag behind the others. Hocart turned to wait, but Rivers waved him on.

They sat down on an overturned tree trunk covered in moss. The sun crashed down, beating the tops of their heads, like somebody hammering tent pegs into the ground. And yet even in these sweaty clothes, the shoulders of his shirt thickly encrusted with bat droppings, Rivers had the same feeling of being new, unsheathed.

They sat tranquilly, side by side, in no hurry to begin the mangled business of communication. A slight breeze cooled their skin.

'*Tongo polo,*' Rivers said at last, because that's where they'd left off. How long? he asked again. How many days?

A bright, amused, unmistakably affectionate look from Njiru. There was no fixed time, he said, though eighteen days was common. His grandmother had observed *tongo polo* for two hundred days, but that was exceptional because Homu, his grandfather, had been a great chief. The men of Roviana blew the conch for her.

Blew the conch? Rivers asked. What did that mean?

A short silence, though not, Rivers thought, indicating a reluctance to go on speaking. At that moment Njiru would have told him anything. Perhaps this was the result of that time in the cave when they'd reached out and gripped each other's hands. No, he thought. *No.* There had been *two* experiences in the cave, and he was quite certain Njiru shared in both. One was the reaching out to grasp each other's hands. But the other was a shrinking, no, no, not shrinking, a *compression* of identity into a single hard unassailable point: the point at which no further compromise is possible, where nothing remains except pure naked self-assertion. The right to be and to be *as one is.*

Njiru's grandfather, Homu, was famous for having taken ninety-three heads in a single afternoon. Through his grandmother he was related to Inkava, who, until the British destroyed his stronghold, had been the most ferocious of the great head-hunting chiefs of Roviana. This was his inheritance. Rivers glanced sideways at him, close enough to see how the white lime flaked on the taut skin of his cheekbones. Njiru was speaking, not out of friendship – though he felt friendship – but out of that hard core of identity, no longer concerned to evade questions or disguise his pride in the culture of his people.

The blowing of the conch, he said, signifies the completion of a successful raid. He turned and looked directly at Rivers. The widow of a chief can be freed only by the taking of a head.

ELEVEN

Monday, 16 September 1918

We live in tamboos – a sort of cross between a cowshed and an outdoor privy. Corrugated iron walls and roof – bloody noisy when it rains, and it's raining now – carpeted with straw that rustles and smells and gleams in the candle-light. Fields outside – perfectly reasonable fields when we arrived. Now, after last night's heavy rain and the constant churning of boots and wheels, there's a depth of about eighteen inches of mud. The duckboards are starting to sink. Oh, and it gets into everything. The inside of my sleeping-bag is *not* inviting – I was tempted to sleep outside it last night. *But*. Mustn't complain. (Why not? The entire army survives on grousing.) In fact mud and duckboards are about the only familiar things left.

I've got a permanent feeling of *wrongness* at the nape of my neck. Exposure's the right word, I suppose, and for once the army's bad joke of a haircut isn't to blame. We're out in the open all the time and

I'm used to a war where one scurries about below ground like a mole or a rat. (Rats thrived on us — literally. We must have devastated the moles.) It occurred to me last night that Rivers's idea of my using myself as a test case — the football he told me to dribble across — has one fundamental flaw in it. Same loony — different war. As far as I can make out, Rivers's theory is that the crucial factor in accounting for the vast number of breakdowns this war has produced is not the horrors — war's always produced plenty of those — but the fact that the strain has to be borne in conditions of immobility, passivity and helplessness. Cramped in holes in the ground waiting for the next random shell to put you out. If that *is* the crucial factor, then the test's invalid — because every exercise we do now is designed to prepare for open, mobile warfare. And that's what's happening — it's all different.

I told Rivers once that the sensation of going over the top was sexy. I don't think he believed me, but actually there *was* something in common — racing blood, risk, physical exposure, a kind of awful *daring* about it. (Obviously I'm not talking about sex in bed.) But I don't feel anything like that now. There's, *for me*, a nagging, constant apprehension, because I'm out in the open and I know I shouldn't be. New kind of war. The trouble is my nerves are the same old nerves. I'd be happier with a ton or two of France on top of my head.

Day was spent on general clean-up. The men's

reward was compulsory games. I stood obediently on the touchline and yelled and waved. A cold grey day. The ball seemed to fly across the lowering sky like a drenched, heavy, reluctant bird. The men were coated in mud, plumes of steam rising from their mouths. All tremendously competitive, of course – 'C' against 'D' – and curiously unreal. Street-corner football played in the spirit of public-school rugby. I stood and watched my red-faced, red-kneed compatriots charging up and down a social No Man's Land. But at least officers and men play together – it's the only informal contact there is outside the line.

At half-time some of them stripped off their shirts and the steam rose from their bodies, red and white, chapped hands and faces, as they stood panting. Jenkins waved at somebody off the pitch and for a moment his face was turned towards me, greenish eyes, red hair, milky white skin blotched with freckles, I had to make an effort to look away. Mustn't get the reputation of 'having an eye for Tommy'. Bad for discipline. Though I don't know what the fuck else there is to look at.

That's the other change: the men's expressions. That look on Jenkins's face as he turned to wave. Before, there were basically two expressions. One you saw at Étaples, the rabbit-locked-up-with-a-stoat look. I've only ever seen that expression in one other place, and that was the Royces' house. Family of four boys in the next street to us. Their father used to make them line up every night after he'd had a few pints, and lift their shirt-tails. Then he'd thrash them with a ruler on their bare bums. Every night without fail. One of them asked once, 'What's it for, Dad?' And he said, 'It's for whatever you've done that you think you've got away with.' But my God they could fight. One of them was the bane of my life at school.

The other expression was the trench expression. It looks quite daunting if you don't know what it is. Any one of my platoon could have posed for a propaganda poster of the Brutal Hun, but it wasn't brutality or anything like that. It was a sort of *morose disgust*, and it came from living in trenches that had bits of human bone sticking out of the walls, in freezing weather corpses propped up on the fire step, flooded latrines.

Whatever happens to us it can't be as bad as that.

Wednesday, 18 September

Today we went to the divisional baths, which are in a huge, low barn. For once it was sunny and dry and the march, though long, was not too tiring. They weren't ready for us and the men sat on the grass outside and waited, leaning on each other's knees or stretched out on the grass with their arms behind their heads. Then it was their turn.

The usual rows of rain butts, wine barrels, a couple of old baths (proper baths). The water any temperature from boiling to tepid depending on where you were in the queue. They take off their clothes, leave them in piles, line up naked, larking about, jostling, a lot of jokes, a few songs, everybody happy because it's not the dreary routine of drills and training. Inside the barn, hundreds of tiny chinks of sunlight from gaps in the walls and roof, so the light shimmers like shot silk, and these gleams dance over everything, brown faces and necks, white bodies, the dividing line round the throat sharp as a guillotine.

One of my problems with the baths is that I'm always dressed. Officers bathe separately. And . . . Well, it's odd. One of the things I like sexually, one of the things I fantasize about, is simply being fully dressed with a naked lover, holding him or her from behind. And what I feel (apart from the obvious) is great tenderness – the sort of tenderness that depends on being more powerful, and that is really, I suppose, just the acceptable face of sadism.

This doesn't matter with a lover, where it's just a game, but here the disproportion of power is real and the nakedness involuntary. Nothing to be done about it. I mean, I can scarcely trip about with downcast eyes like a maiden aunt at a leek show. But I feel uncomfortable, and I suspect most of the other officers don't.

Through the barn, out into the open air, dressing in clean clothes, a variety of drawers and vests, most of them too big. The army orders these things to fit the Sons of Empire, but some of the Sons of Empire didn't get much to eat when they were kids. One of the men in my platoon, barely regulation height, got a pair of drawers he could pull up to his chin. He paraded around, laughing at himself, not minding in the least when everybody else laughed too.

Watching him, it suddenly struck me that soldiers' nakedness has a quality of pathos, not merely because the body is so obviously vulnerable, but because they put on indignity and anonymity with their clothes, and for most people, civilians, most of the time, the reverse is true.

March back very cheerful, everybody singing, lice eggs popping in the seams of the clean clothes as soon as the bodies warm them through. But we're used to that. And I started thinking – there's a lot of time to think on marches – about Father Mackenzie's church, the huge shadowy crucifix on the rood screen dominating everything, a sheaf of hollyhocks lying in the chancel waiting to be arranged, their long stems scrawling wet across the floor. And behind every altar, blood, torture, death. St John's head on a platter, Salome offering it to Herodias, the women's white arms a sort of cage around the severed head with its glazed eyes. Christ at the whipping block, his expression distinctly familiar. St Sebastian hamming it up and my old friend St Lawrence on his grid. Father Mackenzie's voice booming from the vestry. He loved me, the poor sod, I really think he did.

And I thought about the rows of bare bodies

lining up for the baths, and I thought it isn't just me. Whole bloody western front's a wanker's paradise. This is what they've been praying for, this is what they've been longing for, for years. Rivers would say something sane and humorous and sensible at this point, but I stand by it and anyway Rivers isn't here. Whenever a man with a fuckable arse hoves into view you can be quite certain something perfectly dreadful's going to happen.

But then, something perfectly dreadful *is* going to happen. So that's all right.

Sunday, 22 September

Morning – about the nearest we ever get to a lie-in (I've been up and on the go by 5. 30 every day this week). Wyatt's shaving and there's a voluntary service starting just outside. Smell of bacon frying, sound of pots and pans clattering about and Longstaffe whistling as he cleans my boots. Hallet's on the other side of the table writing to his fiancée, something that always takes *hours* and *hours*. And the rain's stopped and there's a shaft of sunlight on the ground and the straw looks like gold. The razor rattling against the side of the bowl makes a pleasant sound. The ghost of Sunday Morning at home – roast beef and gravy, the windows steamed up, the *News of the World* rustling as Dad drops half of it, the Sally Army tuning up outside.

> Onward, Christian soldiers,
> Marching as to war,
> With the cross of Jesus
> Going on before.

Twenty – perhaps a few more – male voices in unison. Longstaffe's singing the alternative version:

> Forward Joe Soap's army
> Marching without fear
> With your brave commander
> Safely in the rear.

> He boasts and skites
> From morn till night
> And thinks he's very brave,
> But the men who really did the job
> Are dead and in their grave.

Sung very cheerfully with great good humour. We're all looking forward to Sunday dinner, which is roast beef and roast potatoes. I'm famished. And there is *not* going to be a gas drill during this meal. I *know*.

Tuesday, 24 September

Bussed forward. Men sang all the way, in high spirits, mainly I think because they didn't have to march.

Thursday, 26 September

The nearest village is in ruins. Extraordinary jagged shapes of broken walls in moonlight, silver mountains and chasms, with here and there black pits of craters thronged with weeds.

Some of the other villages aren't even ruins. You're not supposed to mention the effects of enemy fire, but a lot of this is the effect of British fire so perhaps I *can* mention it. Nothing's left. We passed through one village that hadn't a single wall above knee height. Old trenches everywhere, tangles of rusting barbed-wire, rib-cages of horses that rotted where they fell. And worse and worse.

The men, except for the one or two I remember from last year, are still reserved. Sometimes when they're alone at night you hear laughter. Not often. They guard the little privacy they have jealously. Most of the 'devotion' people talk about is from officers – *some* of the officers – to the men. I don't myself see much sign that it's reciprocated. If they trust anybody they trust the NCOs, who're older, for the most part, and come from the same background. But then I wasn't born to the delusion that I'm responsible for them.

What I am responsible for is GAS. Either the Adjutant wasn't joking or if he was it's a continuing joke. My old nickname – the Canary – has been revived. Owen for some reason is known as the

Ghost. Evidently when he disappeared into Craiglock-hart – and I suspect didn't write to anybody because he was ashamed (I didn't either) – they concluded he was dead.

Gas drill happens several times a day. The routine lectures aren't resented too much (except by me – I have to give them), but the random drills are hated by everybody. You're settling down for the night, or about to score a goal, or raising the first forkful of hot food to your lips, and *wham*! Rattles whirl, masks are pulled on, arms and fists pumped, and then the muffled hollow shout GAS! GAS! GAS! Creatures with huge eyes like insects flicker between the trees. What they hate – what *I* hate – is the gas drill that comes while you're marching or doing PT or bayonet training, because then you have to go on, flailing about in green light, with the sound of your breathing – In. Out. In. Out. – drowning all other sounds. And every movement leeches energy away.

Nobody likes the mask. But what I have to do is watch out for the occasional man who just can't cope with it at all, who panics as soon as it comes down over his head. And unfortunately I think I've found one, though he's in my company which means I can keep an eye on him.

The attitude to gas has changed. It's used more and feared less. A few of the men are positively gas happy. OK, they think, if a whiff or two gets you back to base and doesn't kill you, why not? It's become the equivalent of shooting yourself in the foot and a lot harder to detect.

At dinner I told Hallet and Potts that four years ago we were told to protect ourselves from gas by pissing on our socks. You folded one sock into a pad and used the other to tie it over your mouth and nose. They gaped at me, not sure if I was serious or not. 'Did it work?' asked Hallet. 'No,' I said. 'But it didn't half take your mind off it.' And they both laughed, quite relieved, I think, to know I was only having them on.

It used to give you spots round your mouth. Not that that was our main worry at the time.

And today was pay day. After an afternoon spent crawling running falling crawling again across wet fields, the men were so caked in mud they looked as if they were made of it. Tired, but pay day's always good, even if you've nothing to spend it on, and they were chattering, jostling, laughing as they queued. Then the rattles whirred. A groan went up – (with the real thing there isn't time to groan – more practice needed) and then the usual routine: clenched fists, pumping arms, GAS! GAS! GAS!

They went on queuing. Mud-brown men standing in mud, the slanting rays of the sun gilding the backs of their hands, the only flesh now visible. I was sitting next to Hardwick, ticking off names on the list. One man, waiting immediately behind the man who was being paid, turned his face a little to one side, and I saw, in those huge insect eyes, not one but two setting suns.

Friday, 28 September

Since yesterday evening there's been a continuous bombardment. All the roads forward are choked, drivers stuck in the mud, swearing at each other, a flickering greenish-yellow light in the sky and every now and then the whine and thud of a shell. A constant drone of planes overhead, all going one way.

We move forward tonight.

TWELVE

Rivers walked along the path between the tent and Narovo village, the full moon casting his shadow ahead of him. All around were the scuffles and squeals of the bush, the scream of some bird that turned into a laugh, then silence for a moment, more scuffles, more squeals, the night-long frenzy of killing and eating.

Once in the village he went straight to Ngea's hall, stooped and went in. The scare ghost shivered at his approach.

The women were asleep, the widows who tended Emele. He tiptoed past them, and knelt down, calling, 'Emele! Emele!', an urgent whisper that caused one of the widows to stir and mutter in her sleep. He waited till she settled before he called the name again. When there was no reply he pushed the door open and there, curled up in the prescribed position, back bent, hands resting on her feet, was Kath.

'Kath, Kath,' he said. 'What on earth are you

doing here?' And the movement of his lips woke him up.

He sat on the edge of the bed, peering at his watch. Four o'clock, never a good time to wake. His throat was very sore. He swallowed several times, and decided what was needed was that good old medical stand-by, a glass of water.

In the bathroom he blinked in the white light, caught a glimpse of himself in the looking-glass and thought, My God, is this really what you've done to yourself? He took a moment to contemplate baggy eyes and thinning hair, but he wasn't sunk so deep in neurosis or narcissism as to believe an overhead light at four a. m. lays bare the soul. He drank a glass of water and went back to bed.

Despite the hour the curtains let in a little light, starlight, he supposed, there was no moon tonight. It was curiously reminiscent of the light in the tent on Eddystone. He beat the pillows into a more comfortable shape, and tried to get back to sleep.

'Leave the flap open,' Rivers said.

It had been hotter than usual, an oven of a day in which people and trees had shimmered like reflections in water. The earth outside the tent was baked hard. He watched a line of red ants struggle across the immensity, a group at the rear carrying a dead beetle many times their own size.

Hocart emerged from the tent. 'I don't think I can face sleeping in there tonight.'

'We can sleep out here if you like. As long as you're careful with the net.'

The remains of their evening meal lay on the table. Neither of them had felt like eating much.

'What do we do?' Hocart said, sitting cross-legged on the ground beside Rivers. 'What do we do if they come back with a head? Or *heads*, God help us.'

Rivers said slowly, 'Logically, we don't intervene.'

'Logically, we're dead. Even if we decide we won't tell the authorities, how do they know we won't? From their point of view, the only safe thing to do is –'

'Obey the law.'

'Get rid of us.'

'I don't think they'll do that.'

'Could they?'

'Well, yes, probably. The point is, it won't happen, there isn't going to be a head.'

'But if –'

'If there is we'll deal with it.'

A long, stubborn, unconvinced silence from Hocart.

'Look, you know what the penalties are. If they go on a raid there's no way the British Commissioner isn't going to hear about it. And then you've got a gunboat off the coast, villages on fire, trees cut down, crops destroyed, pigs killed. Screaming women and children driven into the bush. You *know* what happens.'

'Makes you proud to be British, doesn't it?'

'Are you suggesting head-hunting should be allowed?'

'No.' Tight-lipped.

'Good. When these people were taking heads they virtually depopulated Ysabel. It *had* to be stopped.'

'So how are they going to get her out?'

Rivers hesitated. 'I don't know. She can't stay in there for ever.'

What he secretly thought, but was superstitiously afraid of saying, was that the situation would end in Emele's suicide. He could see no other way out.

The following morning he went to see Namboko Taru. She'd become very fond of him (and he of her) ever since his miming of alternating constipation and diarrhoea had kept her amused while Njiru removed the *nggasin* from her belly.

She and her friend Namboko Nali had been bathing in the sea and their hair smelled of salt water. Taru's scrawny brown arms were folded across her breasts as she sat, with her back against the wall of her hut, steaming gently in the sun, while hens stepped delicately around her, pecking the dust. He sat beside her, admiring the gleam of dull emerald in the cockerel's neck feathers, as the village came slowly to life.

After a few minutes' gossip he started asking her about love charms, the subject they'd talked about at their last meeting. Three other women came out and listened. He got out his notebook and took down the words of the charm Taru supplied, aware that more than the usual amount of whispering and giggling was going on. Taru offered him betel to chew, and thinking, What the hell, who needs teeth? he accepted it. The women giggled again. A little while later Taru offered him lime, and to humour her he let her draw white lines on his cheekbones. The giggling was now almost out of control, but he pressed on to the end of the charm, at which point it was revealed that the words only became efficacious if the man accepted betel and lime from the woman's basket.

He laughed with them, and by the time they'd finished they were on such terms that he felt he could ask them anything. Even about Emele and *tongo polo*. Taru vehemently denied there was any question of suicide. Suicide, *ungi*, was totally different. Taru and Nali had helped Kera, the widow of the previous chief, to kill herself. She had tried poisoning herself with tobacco and that hadn't worked. And then she'd tried to hang herself, but the bough had broken. So they'd held a pole for her, high above their heads, and she'd twined a strip of calico round her throat and hanged herself from the pole. Garrotted more like, Rivers thought. It would not have been a quick or an easy death. What decided whether the widow would *ungi* or observe *tongo polo*? he asked. It was her choice, they said.

Returning to the tent, he found Hocart lying outside, having spent the first part of the morning washing clothes. He was asleep, or resting, with his arms across his face shielding his eyes from the sun. Rivers put his foot on his chest and pressed lightly.

Hocart peered up at him, taking in the white lines on his face. '*My God.*'

'I think I just got engaged.'

A bubble of laughter shook Hocart's ribs. 'Lucky woman.'

Sleeping was difficult, because of the heat, even after they'd taken their beds outside the tent. Sometimes they gave up altogether, and went to lie in the shallows, where the small waves, gleaming with phosphorescent light, broke over them.

Rivers had become obsessed by Emele. Wherever he was, whatever he was doing, the thought of the woman cramped inside the enclosure, inside the hut, followed him until he saw every other aspect of life on the island in the shadow of her imprisonment.

In the mornings he would go down to bathe and watch the canoes go out, foam flashing from the paddles, a wordless song drifting across the water: '*Aie, aie, aie.*' All vowel sounds, it seemed to be, no consonants. And then the smack of water being slapped to lure bonito into the nets.

It was still idyllic. His own happiness did not lessen, but always, now, there were these two points of darkness: Emele cramped in her enclosure; Ngea rotting in his *era*. Once he walked up the path on the other side of the beach, unable to explain his desire to see Ngea, for the facts of physical decomposition neither fascinated nor frightened him. A corpse was something one buried or dissected. Nothing more. And yet he needed to see Ngea.

The smell reached him when he was no more than half way up the path. He pinched his nostrils, breathing through his open mouth, but even so a few yards further on he had to abandon the attempt. A black cloud of flies, so dense it looked solid, rose at his approach, heat made audible. He backed away, as much as anything because they reminded him of the bats in the cave, and that experience, the sense of being unshelled, peeled in some way, that had seemed so positive at the time, now made him afraid. He was open to whatever might happen in this place, open in the way that a child is, since no previous experience was relevant.

The heat continued. From mid-afternoon onwards there was a curious bronze light in the sky, which became brownish towards evening, as if even the air were singed. Occasional flicks of wind teased the outermost branches of the trees, but did not disturb the intense brooding stillness.

Rivers slept uneasily, waking finally at 'fowl-he-sing-out', aware of having heard a new and different sound. He lay and listened and was just about to turn over and try to snatch an extra hour when it came again: the brazen blare of a conch shell.

He was on his feet and outside the tent in a matter of minutes. The bush distorted sounds, bouncing echoes back, but then he was aware of the crash of hurrying footsteps through the undergrowth, people running down to the beach. He shook Hocart awake, and followed the crowd, holding back a little, not knowing how secret this was, or how much it might matter that he was witnessing it.

He saw Njiru at the water's edge, draped in a white cloth, with a staff in his hand, looking out over the bay.

A canoe was heading in, quickly, paddled by Lembu, and in the stern was a bundle of some kind. He was too far away to see what it was, but an *ah* went up from the crowd, and suddenly, the women and girls began running into the sea, prancing like horses until they reached a depth where they could cast themselves forward and swim. Clinging to the canoe's side, they escorted it into the shallow water, and Lembu got out, everything about him shining, teeth, hair, eyes, skin, and hauled the canoe up the beach. He walked back to the stern, unwrapped the bundle, and dragged the contents out on to the sand. A small boy about four years old.

Rivers walked down to the canoe, since nobody seemed to care whether he saw this or not. The child's face was tear-stained, streaked with dirt and snot. He was not actually crying now, though irregular hiccups shook his thin chest. As people surged towards him and stared, he moved closer to his captor, resting one grubby hand on Lembu's naked thigh.

Rivers went up to Njiru. 'Is that your head?' he asked, unaware that he spoke English, not pidgin.

'Yes,' Njiru said steadily.

He took the child from Lembu and, surrounded by excited, smiling people, carried him up the beach path to the village. Rivers followed, but kept well back as the crowd gathered outside Ngea's hall. Lembu blew the conch as they entered the village, and again inside the hall. After a while Emele emerged, hobbling, resting her arms on the shoulders of Taru and Nali. Lembu and Njiru followed her out, and there was general rejoicing, except from the small boy, who stood alone at the centre of the throng, his eyes like black bubbles that at any moment might burst.

THIRTEEN

4 October 1918

What can one say? And yet I've got to write something because however little I remember now I'll remember less in years to come. And it's not true to say one remembers nothing. A lot of it you know you'll never forget, and a few things you'll pray to forget and not be able to. But the connections go. Bubbles break on the surface like they do on the flooded craters round here – the ones that've been here years and have God knows what underneath.

The night of I *think* the 1st (dates go too) we lay all night in a trench one foot deep – the reward of success because this was a *German* trench. Another reward of success was that we had no British troops on our left, we'd raced ahead of them all. I think I'm right in saying we were the only units that broke through the Hindenburg line *and* maintained the position. It was dark, early evening, deep black, and we expected a counter-attack at dawn. Until then there was nothing to do but wait, both intolerably cramped and intolerably exposed, enfilading machine-gun fire on three sides. 'Cramped' isn't a figure of speech either. The trench was hardly more than a scraping in the earth. Any careless movement and you'd had it. And for a lot of the time we wore gas masks, because there'd been a very heavy gas barrage put down by our side and it lingered. The whole area smelled like a failed suicide attempt, and I kept hearing Sarah's voice saying about Johnny, *It was our own gas, our own bloody gas.* In spite of all the drills some of the men were slow to put their masks on, one or two had bad reactions, and then Oakshott decided to have a panic attack. I crawled along to him, not past people, over them, one eel wriggling across the others in the tank, and tried to calm him down. I remember at one point I burst out laughing, can't remember why, but it did me good. There's a kind of angry laughter that gets you back to the centre of yourself. I shared a bar of chocolate with Longstaffe and we huddled together under my great-coat and tried to keep warm. And then the counter-attack came.

Two bubbles break here. Longstaffe sliding back into the trench with a red hole in his forehead and an expression of mild surprise on his face. And the bayonet work. Which I will not remember. Rivers would say, remember *now* – any suppressed memory stores up trouble for the future. Well, too bad. Refusing to think's the only way I can survive and anyway what future?

The whole thing was breakdown territory, as defined by Rivers. Confined space, immobility, helplessness, passivity, constant danger that you can do nothing to avert. But my nerves seem to be all right. Or at least no worse than anybody else's. All our minds are in flight, each man tries to reach his own accommodation with what he saw. What he did. But on the surface it's all jollity. We're marching *back*, through the same desolation, but towards safety. Another battalion has leap-frogged us into the line. And every time my right foot hits the ground I say, *over, over, over*. Because the war's coming to an end, and we all know it, and it's coming to an end partly because of what we did. *We* broke through. *We* held the position.

5 October

I think the worst time was after the counter-attack, when we lay in that trench all day surrounded by the dead. I still had Longstaffe by my side, though his expression changed after death. The look of surprise faded. And we listened to the wounded groaning outside. Two stretcher-bearers volunteered to go out and were hit as soon as they stood up. Another tried later. After that I said, No more, everybody keep down. By nightfall most of the groaning had stopped. A few of the more lightly wounded crawled in under cover of darkness and we patched them up as best we could. But one man kept on and on, it didn't sound like a human being, or even like an animal, a sort of guttural gurgling like a blocked drain.

I decided I ought to try myself, and took Lucas with me. Not like going over the top used to be, *climbing* out of the bloody trench. Just a quick slither through the wire, barbs snagging the sleeves, and into the mud. I felt the coldness on my cheek, and the immense space above, that sense you always get when lying on the ground in the open of the earth as a ball turning in space. There was time to feel this, in spite of the bullets – which anyway frightened me less than the thought of having to see what was making that sound.

The gurgling led us to him. He was lying half way down the side of a flooded crater and the smell of gas was stronger here, as it always is near water. As we started down, bullets peppered the surface, *plop, plop, plop,* an innocent sound like when you skim a flat stone across a river, and bullets flicked the rim where we'd been a second before and sent cascades of loose earth down after us. The gurgling changed as we got closer so he knew something different was happening. I don't think he could have known more than that. I got right up to his feet, and started checking his legs for wounds, nothing, but then I didn't expect it. That sound only comes from a head wound. What made it marginally worse was that the side of the head nearest me was untouched. His whole frame was shaking, his skin blue in the starlight as our skins were too, but his was the deep blue of shock. I said 'Hallet' and for a second the gurgling stopped. I gestured to Lucas and he helped me turn him further over on to his back, and we saw the wound. Brain exposed, a lot of blood, a lot of stuff not blood down the side of the neck. One eye gone. A hole – I was going to say *in* his left cheek – where his left cheek had been. Something was burning, casting an orange light into the sky which reflected down on us. The farm that had been one of our reference points. The underside of the clouds was stained orange by the flames.

We got a rope underneath him and started hauling him round the crater, up the other side, towards our trench and all the time I was thinking, What's the use? He's going to die anyway. I think I thought about killing him. At one point he screamed and I saw the fillings in his back teeth and his mouth filled with blood. After that he was quiet, and it was easier but then a flare went up and everything paled in the trembling light. Bastards, bastards, bastards, I thought. I heard a movement and there on the rim of the crater was a white face looking down. Carter, who, I later discovered, had come out entirely on his own initiative. That was just right. More than three and we'd have been getting in each other's way. We managed to drag him back through fire that was, if anything, lighter than before, though not intentionally I think. Too little mercy had been shown by either side that day for gestures of that sort to be possible.

We fell into the trench, Hallet on top of us. I got something damp on my face that wasn't mud, and brushing it away found a gob of Hallet's brain between my fingertips. Because he'd gone quiet on the last stretch I expected to find him unconscious or dead, but he was neither. I gave him a drink of water. I had to press my hand against his face to get it down, because otherwise it slopped out of the hole. And all the time I was doing it I was thinking, Die can't you? For God's sake, man, just *die*. But he didn't.

When at last we were ordered to pull back I remember peering up at the sky and seeing the stars sparse and pale through a gauze of greenish light, and thinking, Thank God it's evening, because shells were still coming over, and some of them were falling directly on the road. At least we'd be marching towards the relative safety of night.

The sun hung on the lip of the horizon, filling the sky. I don't know whether it was the angle or the drifting smoke that half obscured it, but it was *enormous*. The whole scene looked like something that couldn't be happening on earth, partly the sun, partly the utter lifelessness of the land around us, pitted, scarred, pockmarked with stinking craters and scrawls of barbed-wire. Not even birds, not even carrion feeders. Even the crows have given up. And I stumbled along at the head of the company and I

197

waited for the sun to go down. And the sodding thing didn't. IT ROSE. It wasn't just me. I looked round at the others and I saw the same stupefaction on every face. We hadn't slept for four days. Tiredness like that is another world, just like noise, the noise of a bombardment, isn't like other noise. You see people wade through it, lean into it. I honestly think if the war went on for a hundred years another language would evolve, one that was capable of describing the sound of a bombardment or the buzzing of flies on a hot August day on the Somme. There are no words. There are no words for what I felt when I saw the setting sun rise.

6 October

We're far enough back now for officers from different companies to mess together again. I sit at a rickety little table censoring letters, for the post has arrived, including one for me from Sarah saying she isn't pregnant. I don't know what I feel exactly. I ought to be delighted and of course I am, but that was not the first reaction. There was a split second of something else, before the relief set in.

Letters arrive for the dead. I check names against the list and write *Deceased* in a firm bold hand in the top left-hand corner. Casualties were heavy, not so much in the initial attack as in the counter-attacks.

Gregg died of wounds. I remember him showing

me a letter from home that had big 'kisses' in red crayon from his little girl.

Of the people who shared the house in Amiens only a month ago, Potts is wounded, but likely to live. Jones (Owen's servant) wounded, likely to live. Hallet's wounds are so bad I don't think he can possibly survive. I see him sometimes lying in the lily pond in the garden with the golden fish darting all around him, and silver lines of bubbles on his thighs. More like a pattern than a picture, no depth to it, no perspective, but brilliantly clear. And Longstaffe's dead.

The Thane of Fife had a wife: where is she now?

I look across at Owen, who's doing casualty reports with a Woodbine – now blessedly plentiful again – stuck to his bottom lip, and his hair, rather lank at the moment, flopping over his forehead. For days after the battle he went round with his tunic stiff with blood, but then I had blood and brains on me. We must have stunk like the drains in a slaughter-house, but we've long since stopped smelling each other. He looks like one of the boys you see on street corners in the East End. Open to offers. I must say I wouldn't mind. He looks up, feeling himself the subject of scrutiny, smiles and pushes the fags across. I saw him in the attack, caped and masked in blood, seize a machine-gun and turn it on its previous owners at point-blank range. Like killing fish in a bucket. And I wonder if he sees those faces, grey, open-mouthed faces, life draining out of them before the bullets hit, as I see the faces of the men I killed in the counter-attack. I won't ask. He wouldn't answer if I did. I wouldn't *dare* ask. For the first time it occurs to me that Rivers's job also requires courage.

We don't even mention our own dead. The days pass crowded with meaningless incident, and it's easier to forget. I run the ball of my thumb against the two first fingers of my right hand where a gob of Hallet's brain was, and I don't feel anything very much.

We are Craiglockhart's success stories. *Look at us.* We don't remember, we don't feel, we don't think – at least not beyond the confines of what's needed to do the job. By any proper civilized standard (but what does *that* mean *now*?) we are objects of horror. But our nerves are completely steady. And we are still alive.

PART THREE

FOURTEEN

SHEER FIGHTING
BOTH SIDES PAY THE PRICE
HUNS WAIT FOR THE BAYONET

Prior would have been in that, Rivers thought. He picked the paper up from his breakfast tray and made a real effort to concentrate. It was clear, even from this gung-ho report, that casualties had been heavy. No point checking the casualty lists yet: individual names took at least a week to come through. But he could probably expect a field postcard in the next few days, if Prior was all right. He'd sounded fine in his last letter, but that was ten days ago.

Reading it, Rivers had felt the stab of envy he always experienced on receiving letters from men serving in France. If the wretched war had to happen he'd rather have spent it with Marshall-of-the-Ten-Wounds than with Telford-of-the-Pickled-Penis. He tried to focus on the details of the engagement, but the print blurred before his eyes. And his boiled egg – though God knows what it had cost Mrs Irving to buy – was going down like lead. He really thought he'd be sick if he forced any more of it down. He took his glasses off, put them on the bedside table and pushed the tray away. He meant only to rest a while before starting again, but his fingers slackened and twitched on the counterpane and, after a few minutes, the newspaper with its headlines shrieking about distant battles slipped sighing to the floor.

Ngea's skull, jammed into the *v* of a cleft stick, bleached in the sun. A solitary bluebottle buzzed in and out of the eye sockets and, finding nothing there of interest, sailed away into the blue sky.

On his way down to the beach to bathe, Rivers paused to look at the skull. Only a month ago he'd spoken to this man, had even held his hand briefly on parting. No wonder the islanders wore necklaces of pepeu leaves to guard themselves against *tomate gani yambo*: the Corpse-eating Spirit.

Later the same day he saw the little boy whom Lembu had brought back from Ysabel squatting listlessly outside Njiru's hut, poking about in the dust with a small stick. He was not crying, but he looked dazed. The story was he'd been bought, but Rivers was not inclined to believe it. In these islands – still, in spite of the abolition of head-hunting, warrior communities – not even the poorest family would willingly part with a son. Abduction was more likely. He watched the child for several minutes, wanting to go to him, and yet knowing the appearance of a strange white man would only terrify him more.

'Are they going to kill him?' Hocart said, lying sleepless in bed that night.

'No, they won't do that – they'd have to kill us too.'

'Perhaps that wouldn't worry them.'

'The Commissioner's response to it would.'

But after Hocart was uneasily asleep, twitching and muttering, Rivers lay awake, thinking that if the islanders wanted to get rid of them it wouldn't be too difficult. White men died of blackwater fever all the time, and no doubt there were poisons that mimicked the symptoms. You only had to look at Ngea's skull to know that by the time the next steamer put in there wouldn't be enough of them left to make investigation possible. Moreover, the next steamer would be Brennan's, since he was the local trader, and, confronted by any sign of trouble, he'd simply skedaddle as fast as possible. No, they'd just have to wait and see, and be cautious.

Next morning, when he arrived in the village, the little boy had gone.

They were invited to witness the placing of Ngea's skull in the skull house. Njiru officiated.

At dawn they were woken by the screams of pigs being slaughtered, and all morning columns of smoke had risen from the cooking fires. It was noon before the ceremony started, the sun crashing down on shoulders and heads, the heat intensified by two fires, the sacrificial fire on the hearth in front of the skull house, and the common fire where Rivers and Hocart sat along with people from the village and the surrounding hamlets. Rivers looked out for the small captive boy, but could not see him. Beside him Lembu was plaiting a creeper which he used to tie Ngea's jaw-bone to his skull, before placing a diadem of shells round the cranium and other shells in the sockets of the eyes.

Across the fire, moving figures shimmered in the heat. A woman with a baby in her arms, Nanja, whose own child had died in the confining house and who was now nursing Kwini, the emaciated baby whom Rivers had first seen with Njiru. The child worried at the nipple, guzzling and snuffling – already her wasted thighs had begun to fill out. She would live, he thought, and the idea cheered him for, to western eyes, the stacked-up skulls made disturbing companions.

Njiru raised Ngea's crowned skull above his head, and a silence fell, broken only by the careless cries of the children, but they were some distance away. Rivers could follow most of Njiru's prayer without need of an interpreter. 'We offer pudding, we offer pig, to you the ghosts. Be propitious in war, be propitious in the sea fight, be propitious at the fort, be propitious at the burning of the thatch. Receive the chiefly dead . . .' Here Njiru placed Ngea's skull in the house. 'And be you propitious and smite our enemies, oh, oh, oh!'

It was a prayer for success in the great head-hunting raid that ought to have concluded the mourning for the dead chief. The *Vavolo*, the Night Festival, at which all the young women were free – *tugele* – to all the returning warriors. But the raid would not happen. The prayer could not be answered. Njiru put pork and yam pudding in the sacrificial fire, whose flames burned dull in the sunlight. Then he took the remains of the pudding and walked round the stones that encircled the clearing, placing a mouthful of food on each stone. The stones were called *tomate patu*, stone ghosts, and were erected as memorials to men who died and whose bodies could not be brought home. Rivers watched him go from stone to stone.

Head-hunting had to be banned, and yet the effects of banning it were everywhere apparent in the listlessness and lethargy of the people's lives. Head-hunting was what they had lived for. Though it might seem callous or frivolous to say so, head-hunting had been the most tremendous *fun* and without it life lost almost all its zest.

This was a people perishing from the absence of war. It showed in the genealogies, the decline in the birth rate from one generation to the next – the island's population was less than half what it had been in Rinambesi's youth – and much of that decline was deliberate.

Against the background of such despair might not the temptation of taking one small head in honour of a dead chief prove irresistible? Raids, no, they couldn't do that, the punishment was too severe. But who was to miss one small boy?

Rivers ate the baked yams and pork offered to him, but remained thoughtful. Once he looked up to see Njiru on the other side of the fire, a tall, lean, twisted shape wavering in the column of heat, and surprised on the other man's face an expression of – bitterness? No, stronger than that. Hatred, even.

Kundaite could interpret *talk blong tomate*: the language of ghosts. Sometimes, he said, a meeting was held on the night the old ghosts arrived to take the new ghost back to Sonto with them, and he would question the ghosts and the people would hear them speak. Would this be done for Ngea? Rivers asked. Kundaite didn't know, he wasn't sure, he didn't think so. Would it be done if we give you ten sticks of tobacco? Kundaite nodded. He was given five and promised the other five the following morning. Would they hear Ngea speak? Hocart asked. No, was the reply. 'Ngea he no speak yet. He all same small fellow piccanini.' Kundaite, grasping his tobacco sticks, seemed to be worried. 'Don't tell Njiru,' he said at last.

They all met at sunset in what had been Ngea's hall, and sat cross-legged around the fire. It had been made with green sticks and smoked badly. They coughed, their eyes watered, they waited, nothing happened. Outside it was totally dark, for the moon had not yet risen. Nanja brought in dry sticks, feeding them into the fire skilfully, one by one, until the flames crackled and spurted. Kwini cried and Nanja jiggled and soothed her. Older children sat big-eyed in the firelight, and Rivers felt his own eyelids grow heavy, for he had been up since dawn walking miles in the heat. He blinked hard, making himself look round the circle. Emele – Namboko Emele as she must now be called – was there, wearing brown bark cloth without lime or necklaces. But not Njiru, a surprising absence surely, since he'd placed Ngea's skull in the skull house.

Kundaite came in and sat beside the door in the side of the hut. At a word from him the torches were extinguished, though Rivers could still see people's faces clearly, leaping and shining in the firelight. Silence fell, and deepened, and deepened again. Kundaite closed his eyes and began to moan beneath his breath. Rivers watched him sceptically, wondering whether the attempt to induce a trance state was genuine or merely histrionic. Abruptly, Kundaite seemed to come to himself. He put three sticks of tobacco in the fire as a sacrificial offering, saying casually that the ghosts were on their way from Sonto. A long silence. Nothing happened. Somebody suggested the ghosts were afraid of a dog that was lying by the fire. The animal raised its head on hearing its name, decided there was nothing to worry about and settled down again with a sigh. Others said the ghosts were afraid of the white men.

River's back and thighs were aching from the

squatting position. Suddenly Kundaite said, 'Listen, the canoes.' It was clear, looking round the circle, that they were hearing the swish of paddles. Joy and grief mingled on every face. Emele started the musical wailing characteristic of the women, but stopped when Kundaite held up his hand.

A tense silence. Then somebody whistled. The sound was curiously difficult to locate. Rivers looked round the faces, but could not see who was making the sound. The people began calling out names, familiar to him from the genealogies, each person calling the name of a relative who had recently died. Some not so recently. Namboko Taru called for her grandmother. Then the name Onda was called and somebody whistled again. Rivers could see Hocart also looking round the room, trying to locate the whistler.

A discussion about the white men followed, the ghost's whistles being translated by Kundaite. Who were the white men? Why were they here? Why did they want to hear the language of ghosts? Did the ghosts object to the white men's presence? Kundaite asked. 'What do we do if they say "yes"?' Hocart asked, not moving his lips. 'Get out quick.'

But the ghosts did not object. Onda, whistling, said he had never seen white men. Kundaite pointed to Rivers and Hocart. Onda, apparently satisfied, fell silent. Kundaite's father, also called Kundaite, came next and asked for tobacco. The living Kundaite put his last two sticks in the fire, saying, 'Here is tobacco for you, Kunda. Smoke and depart.' Namboko

Rupe, Ngea's mother, spoke next, saying she had come to take Ngea to Sonto. Other relatives of Ngea followed. At last Kundaite said that Ngea himself was in the room.

A deeper silence fell. Rivers felt the hairs on his arms rise. Namboko Emele began to wail for her husband. Kundaite said, Don't cry. He's going to Sonto. Ngea's mother said, He must go now. He must blow the conch and come to Sonto. By now the room was full of whistles, slithering up and down the walls and all across the floor. At times the sounds seemed almost to be a ripple running across the skin. Namboko Emele began to wail again, and the other women joined in. 'Don't cry,' Ngea's mother said again, through Kundaite's mouth. 'I have come to take him to Sonto.' Then, Kundaite said, Ngea blew the conch. Everybody in the room, except Rivers and Hocart, heard it, and then the whistles faded and there was silence save for the musical wails and cries of the women.

Ten years later, throwing off hot sheets, Rivers reflected that the questions the ghosts had asked had all been questions the living people wanted answered. What *were* the white men doing on the island? *Were* they as harmless as they appeared? *Why* did they want to hear the language of ghosts? *Was* it possible the spirits might be offended by their presence?

At Craiglockhart, Sassoon, trying to decide whether he should abandon his protest and go back to France, had woken to find the ghost of a dead comrade standing by his bed. And thereafter, on more than one occasion, shadowy figures had gathered out of the storm, asking him, Why was he not in the line? Why had he deserted his men?

The ghosts were not an attempt at evasion, Rivers thought, either by Siegfried or by the islanders. Rather, the questions became more insistent, more powerful, for being projected into the mouths of the dead.

Walking back to the tent, a circle of torchlight swaying round their feet, their shoulders bumping as they tried to stay abreast on the narrow path, Rivers and Hocart talked about the seance. A silly word that didn't seem to suit the occasion, but Rivers couldn't think of a better.

'Who was whistling?' Hocart asked.

'I don't know.'

The occasion had moved him in a way he'd never expected when they sat down by that fire. They talked about it for a while, getting the sequence of events clear in their minds, for they had not been able to take notes. Then Rivers said, 'Njiru wasn't there.'

'No, I noticed that.'

Back at the tent Hocart said, 'Shall I light the lamp?'

'No, don't bother. Not for me anyway. I can't wait to get to bed.' He was unbuckling his belt as he spoke, rubbing the skin underneath where trapped sweat prickled. He kicked his trousers to one side and lay down on the bed, only to cry out as his head came into violent contact with something hard and cold. Hocart came in with the torch, his face white behind the beam. On the pillow, indenting it as Rivers's head would have done, was an axe. Rivers picked it up and held it closer to the light. The carving on the handle was rather fine by the standards of the island, and there was a knot, a flaw in the wood, close to the blade.

'Somebody must have left it behind,' Hocart said uncertainly.

'Well, yes, obviously.'

'No, I mean by accident. Whoever it is, he'll be back for it in the morning.'

'I hope not,' Rivers said dryly. 'It's Ngea's.'

'Are you sure?'

Rivers indicated the knot in the wood. 'Yes, I remember this, I noticed it when they put it in the *era* with him.' He stroked the blade. 'No, I'm afraid we've been asking too many awkward questions. We're being warned.'

FIFTEEN

10 October 1918

Back into corrugated iron privies again, which are
dry but in other ways less comfortable than dug-
outs. Owen has somehow managed to stick a portrait
of Siegfried Sassoon to the wall of his. Sassoon in
distinctly Byronic mode, I should say – not the
Sassoon *I* remember, legging it down the main corridor at Craiglockhart with his golf-clubs on his back,
hell-bent on getting out of the place as fast as possible.
I stood and stared, gawped at it. And suddenly I was
back in Rivers's room, watching the late afternoon
sun glint on his glasses during one of his endless
silences. Rivers's silences are not manipulative. (Mine
are. Always.) He's not trying to make you say
more than you want, he's trying to create a safe
space round what you've said already, so you can
think about it without shitting yourself. White net
curtains drifting in on the breeze. *Pok-pok, pok-pok,*
from the tennis courts, until somebody misses and
the rhythm goes.

Owen said, tentatively, something I didn't quite catch. Something to the effect that we 'old Craiglockhartians' must stick together. Once that would have made me puke. I always felt, watching Owen at Craiglockhart, that there was some kind of fantasy going on, that he was having the public-school education he'd missed. I always wanted to say, it's a loonybin, Owen. Who do you think you're kidding? I don't feel that now – perhaps because Craiglockhart was a shared experience of failure, and the past few weeks have expunged it for both of us. Wiped it out in blood, you might say, if you were histrionic, and I am. And not our own blood either.

Would that remark deserve one of Rivers's silences? I don't know. Sometimes I used to think he was back with his fucking head-hunters – he really does love them, his whole face lights up when he talks about them – and that gives him a slightly odd perspective on 'the present conflict' as they say.

I've been recommended for the MC for going out to bring Hallet in. I'd have been like a dog with two tails three years ago. Hallet's still alive, anyway. More than a medal, I wish somebody would just tell me I did the right thing.

11 October

Today we all had to stand up in front of the men and promulgate a new order. 'Peace talk in any form is to cease immediately in the Fourth Army.'

The brass hats needn't worry. Some of the men were sitting on bales of straw cleaning equipment while one read aloud from the paper: Austro-Hungarian Empire collapses, peace imminent, etc. Jenkins, a wizened weasel of a man (*must* be over age, surely), hawked the accumulated phlegm of four long years into his mouth and spat on his rifle. Then he went back to polishing it. Can't think of a better comment.

And yet. And yet. We all, at some level, think we may have made it, we *may* be going to be all right. At any moment now the guns may stop. Oddly enough it doesn't help.

We spend our time in the usual way while 'at rest'. Baths, change of clothes, general clean-up, exercises, compulsory games, church parade. Oh, and of course, *gas drills*. A lot of the men are coughing and hoicking and wheezing because they were slow putting on their masks. And perhaps deliberately in some cases; perhaps some people thought they'd get sent back. If so, they've been thoroughly disillusioned, and the proof is the endless cough, cough, cough, cough that accompanies all other activities. Owen irritated me profoundly by saying it was their own fault. He put *his* mask on in time, he's all right, he says. I'm afraid I let fly. The only person round here who has the right to be smug about surviving a gas attack is me. ME.

When we got here we found a new draft had arrived from Scarborough. They're sitting around at the moment, expecting to be welcomed, though so far they haven't been. Difficult to say why the other men avoid them, but they do. Heads too full of battle to be able to cope with all those clean, innocent, *pink* faces. A couple of them I remember. One particularly useless boy, the bane of Owen's life at the Clarence Gardens Hotel, until he upset some hot soup in the CO's lap, after which everybody, including Owen, found him a lot more tolerable. Waiters, drummer boys. They sit around, when they're not being chivvied from one place to another, most of them dejected, miserable. Frightened. A few strut up and down – hard men – real killers – and succeed only in looking even more like baby thrushes than the rest.

12 October

Parcels arrived today. Shared out fags in parcels intended for the dead and wounded. Tempers immediately improved. A lot of niggling administrative jobs connected with feeding men from the new draft into the companies. Get flashes from the battle while

I'm filling in forms. The man I bayoneted. What worries me is that he was middle aged. Odd really – it's supposed to be golden youth you mourn for. But he was so obviously somebody who should have been at home, watching his kids grow up, wondering whether brushing his hair over the bald patch would make it more or less obvious, grumbling about the price of beer. And yes, you *could* see all this in his face – with some people you can. Some people do look exactly what they are. *Fuck it.*

Meanwhile more exercises. Route marches. We feed our faces on precisely adequate quantities of horrible food. Bread now has potatoes in it. (Makes an interesting combination with the wood chippings.)

15 October

Last night we were entertained by The Peddlers, the whole battalion, and a few officers invited over from our neighbours on the left. Among whom was Marshall-of-the-Ten-Wounds, now acting Lt Colonel, who applauded every turn with childlike glee. Exactly what you wouldn't expect him to do. At the end of the evening, when things are allowed to get a bit slushy, somebody sang 'Rose of England':

> Rose of England breathing England's air,
> Flower of liberty beyond compare.

Not a bad voice – it soared over the privies and the

tents, the columns of smoke from the fires – and I looked along the row and there was Marshall with great big fat tears rolling down his cheeks. I envied him.

16 October

Bainbrigge's dead. I remember him in the oyster bar in Scarborough a couple of nights before we left. We were all pissed, but Bainbrigge was pissed enough to quote his own poems (than which there is no pisseder). He was talking to Owen, saying real anti-war poems ought to celebrate what war deprives men of – wait for it – 'Beethoven, Botticelli, beer and boys.' Owen kicked him under the table, for my benefit, I think. A wasted kick.

More new arrivals from England yesterday. And I've been transferred to a tent, just as the weather's laying on the first real taste of winter. The misery of sleety rain under canvas. Not that we spend much time under it. We're out all day doing route marches, column into line, consolidation, etc., etc. And gas drills.

But now it's evening. The men are leaning against their packs or each other's knees, aching legs allowed to sprawl at last, writing to wives, mothers, girl-friends. Perhaps even one or two to Beethoven & Co. I said I wasn't born to the delusion that I'm responsible for them. True. (True I wasn't born to it, true it's a delusion.) But I wouldn't like it to be thought I didn't care. So. Going round the group nearest to me. Wilson's got a fucking great nail sticking up through the heel of his left boot. We've all had a go at it: hammers, pliers, tent pegs, God knows what. Still it sticks up, and since it breaks the skin he's quite likely to get a septic sore, unless I can find him another pair of boots. Which ought to be easy, but isn't. Unfortunately, the septic sore won't be enough to get him out of the line if we have to go back there. It'll just exhaust him, make every step a greater misery than it need be.

Oakshott, who's sort of on the fringes of the group – he's taken to not talking to people – is well on the way to cracking up. (I should know.) The thing is he's *not* windy, he's a perfectly good soldier, no more than reasonably afraid of rifle and machine-gun bullets, shells, grenades. (Let's not ask ourselves how afraid that is.) He isn't even windy about gas, though inevitably it comes across like that. He's just terrified of the *mask*. I don't know what to do with him. Once or twice recently I've noticed him lagging behind in gas drills, and I've noticed myself letting him get away with it. Which I mustn't do. If *he* gets away with it, they'll all start.

Next to him, in front of him rather, is Moore. Moore's wife spent the evening of the Friday before last in the lounge bar of the Rose and Crown (I know it well) in the company of one Jack Puddephat, who has a good job at the munitions factory (same one Dad works at) and brings home five quid a week. Moore's sister-in-law, a public-spirited soul, was kind enough to write and tell him about it.

Heywood's kid has tonsillitis and the doctor's all for whipping them out. Heywood's all for leaving well alone, but the letter he's writing now won't get there in time.

Buxton's missus is expecting their first. The birth doesn't seem to worry her, but it terrifies him. His own mother died in childbirth, and he's convinced himself the same thing's going to happen to her.

Jenkins writes the most incredibly passionate love letters to his wife. They've been married since before the Flood, but obviously nothing's faded. I get erections reading them. Nothing else I've done sexually has filled me with such shame. In fact it's the only thing that's ever filled me with *any* shame. He *must* know they're censored, and yet still he writes, page after page. Perhaps he needs to say it so much he somehow manages to forget that I read them first? It's the mental equivalent of the baths. Here I sit, fully clothed as it were, knowing my letters to Sarah *won't* be censored. I suppose random checks are carried out on officers' letters, but at least it's done somewhere else, and not by people you have to see every day.

Peace talk goes on whether orders forbidding it are promulgated or no. On the night we heard the Germans had agreed to peace talks there was a great impromptu party, officers and men together.

Everybody sang. And then next day in *John Bull* there's Bottomley saying, No, no, no and once again no. We must fight to the bitter end. (*Whose* end?) *I don't want any more talk about not being out to destroy the German nation – that is just what I am out for . . .*

But it doesn't wash with the men. Not this time. In fact some of them have taken to going to the latrines waving copies of *John Bull*.

Nobody here sees the point of going on now.

18 October

But others do. We leave here today, going back into the line.

SIXTEEN

October rain spattered the glass. Outside in Vincent Square golden leaves were trodden in the mud. Rivers stopped coughing, put his handkerchief away, and apologized.

''S all right,' Wansbeck said. 'I should be apologizing to you. I gave it you.'

'At least I can't give it back,' Rivers said, wiping his eyes. 'In fact you and I are about the only two round here who can't get it.'

'Things are getting pretty bad, aren't they? I mean, on the wards. I don't suppose I could do anything to help?'

Rivers looked blank.

'Lifting patients. It just seems bloody ridiculous a great big chap like me sitting around doing nothing while some poor little nurse struggles to lift a twelve-stone man on her own.'

'It's very kind of you,' Rivers said carefully. 'But I really don't think the authorities would allow it. In any case you're not doing "nothing".'

Silence. The hint was not taken up. Rivers forced himself to open his shoulders, knowing his tension was communicating itself to Wansbeck, though it was only the tension of driving himself through a long day while still feeling very far from well. 'How have you been?'

'Smell's gone.' A flicker of amusement. 'I know it wasn't there, but it's still nice to be rid of it.'

'Hmm, good.' What pleased Rivers even more than the vanished smell was the hint of self-mockery. The one expression you never see on the faces of the mentally ill. 'When did that happen?'

'Just faded gradually. I suppose about the middle of last week I suddenly realized I wasn't worried about it any more.'

'And the dream?'

'It isn't a dream.'

'The apparition, then.'

'Oh, we still see quite a bit of each other.'

'Do you ever miss a night?'

A faint smile. 'You mean, does *he* ever miss a night? No.'

A long silence. Rivers said, 'It's difficult, isn't it, to talk about . . . beliefs?'

'Is it?'

'I find it so.'

Wansbeck smiled. 'What a very honest man you are.'

'I wanted to ask if you believe in life after death?'

A groan, followed by silence.

It *is* difficult, Rivers thought. He could list all the taboo topics on Eddystone, but in his own society it seemed to him the taboos had shifted quite considerably in recent years. It was almost easier now to ask a man about his private life than to ask what beliefs he lived by. Before the war . . . but one must beware of attributing everything to the war. The change had started years before the war.

'No,' Wansbeck said at last.

'You had to think.'

'Yes, well, I used to believe in it. I was brought up to. I suppose one doesn't like to have to admit it's gone. Faith.'

'What changed your mind?'

A flare of the eyebrows. Rivers waited.

'Corpses. Especially in cold weather when they couldn't be buried. And in summer in No Man's Land. The flies buzzing.'

They rose from Ngea's body in a black cloud.

'It needn't have that effect, though, need it? What about priests keeping a model of a skull on their desks? Because it reminds them of their faith.'

Or Njiru. Man he stink, he rotten, bymby he go Sonto. A simple, casual statement of fact.

'Well, that's the effect it had on *me*. I'd like to believe. I'd like to believe in the possibility of – you're right, it *is* embarrassing – redemption.'

Silence.

'Anyway,' Rivers said, when it became clear there

would be no more, 'you don't believe that the apparition is the man you killed? You don't believe it's his ghost?'

'No, though I'm not sure I'd believe that even if I were still a Christian.'

'So what is it?'

'A projection of my own mind.'

'Of your guilt?'

'*No.* Guilt's what I feel sitting here, I don't need an apparition. No, it's . . .' A deep sigh. 'Guilt as objective fact — not guilt as *feeling*. It's not . . . well, I was going to say it's not subjective, but of course it has to be, doesn't it?'

'It's the representation to yourself of external standards that *you* believe to be valid?'

'Yes.'

'What language does it speak?'

A blank look. 'Doesn't. Doesn't speak.'

'What language would it speak if it spoke? Yes, I know it's an irrational question but then the apparition isn't rational either. What language would —'

'English. Has to be.'

'So why don't you speak to it?'

'It's only there for a second.'

'That's not the way you described it. You said it was endless.'

'All right, it's an endless second.'

'You should be able to say a lot, then.'

'Tell it my life story?'

Rivers said gently, 'It knows your life story.'

Wansbeck was thinking deeply. 'All right. It's bloody mad, but I'll have a go.'

'What will you say?'

'I have absolutely no idea.'

After Wansbeck had gone, Rivers sat quietly for a few minutes before adding a note to the file. Sassoon had been much in his mind while he was speaking to Wansbeck, Sassoon and the apparitions that gathered round his bed and demanded to know why he was not in France. Also, another of his patients at Craiglockhart, Harrington, who'd had dreadful nightmares, even by Craiglockhart standards, and the nightmares had continued into the semi-waking state, so that they acquired the character of hypnagogic hallucinations. He saw the severed head, torso and limbs of a dismembered body hurtling towards him out of the darkness. A variant of this was a face bending over him, the lips, nose and eyelids eaten away as if by leprosy. The face, in so far as it was identifiable at all, was the face of a close friend whom Harrington had seen blown to pieces. From these dreams he woke either vomiting or with a wet bed, or both.

At the time he witnessed his friend's death Harrington had already been suffering from headaches, split vision, nausea, vomiting, disorder of micturition, spells of forgetfulness and a persistent gross tremor of the hands, dating from an explosion two months before in which he'd been buried alive. Despite these symptoms he had remained on duty (shoot the MO, thought Rivers) until his friend's death precipitated a total collapse.

What was interesting about Harrington was that instead of treatment bringing about an elaboration of the nightmares, so that the horrors began to assume a more symbolic, less directly representational form – the normal path to recovery – something rather more remarkable had happened. His friend's body had begun to reassemble itself. Night after night the eaten-away features had fleshed out again. And Harrington talked to him. Long conversations, apparently, or they seemed long to him on waking, telling his friend about Rivers, about life at Craiglockhart, about the treatment he was receiving . . .

After several weeks of this, he awoke one day with his memory of the first hour after the explosion restored. He had, even in his traumatized state and under heavy fire, crawled round the pieces of his friend's body collecting items of equipment – belt, revolver, cap and lapel badges – to send to the mother. The knowledge that, far from having fled from the scene, he had behaved with exemplary courage and loyalty, did a great deal to restore Harrington's self-esteem, for, like most of the patients at Craiglockhart, he suffered from a deep sense of shame and failure. From then on the improvement was dramatic, though still the conversations with the dead friend continued, until one morning he awoke crying, and realized he was crying, not only for his own loss but also for his friend's, for the unlived years.

Wansbeck's predicament was worse than either of these cases. Siegfried's apparitions vanished as soon as he agreed to give up his protest and go back to France. The external demands the nocturnal visitors represented, and which Siegfried himself believed to be valid, had been met. Harrington had been enormously helped by the discovery that he'd behaved better than he thought he had. From that moment on, his recovery had been one of the most dramatic Rivers could recall. Neither of these outcomes was available to Wansbeck, who'd fought a perfectly honourable war until one action had made him in his own eyes – and in the eyes of the law – a criminal. Almost everything one could say to console him either obscenely glossed over the offence or was in some other way insulting, and would have been instantly recognized as such by Wansbeck. A lesser man would have borne this better.

Rivers wondered whether Sassoon and Harrington had been *too* much in the forefront of his mind while he was listening to Wansbeck. At best, on such occasions, one became a conduit whereby one man's hard-won experience of self-healing was made available to another. At worst, one no longer listened attentively enough to the individual voice. There was a real danger, he thought, that in the end the stories would become one story, the voices blend into a single cry of pain.

And he was tired. Because of the flu epidemic he'd been on duty for thirty of the last forty-eight hours and he was on duty again tonight too. Sighing, he reached for an envelope, took out an X-ray and clipped it to the screen.

A skull stared out at him. He stood back and looked at it for a moment, one lens of his glasses illumined by the lighted screen, the other reflecting the rainy light of a November afternoon. Then he reached for the notes.

Second Lieutenant Matthew Hallet, aged twenty, admitted 18 October with bullet wounds to the head and to the lower jaw. On admission he was incapable of giving an account of his injuries, and the only information brought with him was a small card saying he had been wounded on 30 September.

So he was now twenty days post-injury.

A rifle bullet had entered just to the left of the inner canthus of the right ear and had made its exit directly above the insertion of the left ear. The wound of entry was marked by a small perfectly healed scar. The wound of exit consisted of a large irregular opening in the bone and tissues of the scalp, and through this protruded a suppurating hernia cerebri which pulsated.

Oh God.

He had so far said nothing spontaneously. When directly addressed he responded, but his speech was incomprehens-

bile. The wound to his lower jaw made it difficult to determine whether this represented a deficit in the power of using language, or whether the failure to communicate was entirely or primarily mechanical. He showed some under-standing of speech, however, since he had responded to simple questions, when asked to do so, by movements of his unparalysed hand.

Somewhere at the fringe of Rivers's perception was the soft sound of rain continually falling, seeming to seal the hospital away from the darkening afternoon. It had rained incessantly since early morning, the darkness of the day somehow making it even harder to stay awake. He took his glasses off, rubbed his eyes, and turned to the window, where each raindrop caught and held a crescent moon of silver light.

'Do you suppose it's ever going to stop?' Hocart said, turning over restlessly in the gloom of the tent.

It had been raining ever since they'd found Ngea's axe, not restrained English rain but a downpour, a gurgling splatter that flooded into the tent no matter how hard they tried to keep it out. Possibly it was stupid to stay inside at all, though difficult not to when even a five-yard dash into the bush to pee meant you came back with hair plastered to your skull and a transparent shirt sticking to your chest.

They lay and watched it through the open flap, a solid wall of water through which the not too distant trees could be glimpsed only dimly, a wavering blue

mass beaten hither and thither by a wind that blew in sudden spiteful squalls. Hocart, in his frustration, had been kicking the roof of the tent where it sloped steeply down over his bed, and his muddy footprints now added to the general squalor and smell. Hot wet bodies, hair washed daily but only in sea water, salt drying to a white scurf on the surface of the skin. The only escape was into the sea, where total immersion relieved the misery of wet.

On the fourth day the rain eased slightly. Rivers stepped out into the clearing and saw Njiru coming along the path towards him, for once without his retinue.

Rivers had been wondering whether to mention the axe, and had decided not to, but as soon as he looked at Njiru he knew it was essential to bring it out into the open.

'Blong you?' he said, holding it out.

'Blong Ngea,' Njiru said, and smiled.

But he took it, putting it into the string basket he carried slung over one shoulder. Rivers heard the chink of one blade on another as it hit Njiru's axe. It was important to be totally steadfast at this moment, Rivers thought. He and Hocart were probably the only white men in the archipelago, apart from the missionaries — *some* of the missionaries — who didn't carry guns. They didn't carry knives either, though on an island covered in dense bush a machete would have been useful. Nothing could possibly be mistaken for a weapon. And they went barefoot, as

the natives did. Harmlessness was their defence, not guaranteed to succeed by any means, but guns would have made the job impossible.

Njiru had come, he said, because one of the oldest skull houses on the island was being rebuilt, and he had to go to say the prayer of purification over the priest. Would Rivers like to go with him? Of course, there was no question.

They set off, Njiru remarking at one point that it always rained when a skull house was being rebuilt because '*tomate* he like bathe all time 'long fresh water'. Soon the narrow path and the steamy heat made conversation impossible. Rivers watched the movement of muscles under the oiled skin, wondering, not for the first time, how much pain Njiru suffered. He was a mystery in many respects and likely to remain so. He was not married, for example, this among a people to whom the concept of celibacy was wholly foreign. Was that because his deformity caused the girls or their parents to regard him as a poor catch? But then in island terms he was both wealthy and powerful. Did he himself feel a disinclination for the married state? And what had the impact been on a small crippled boy of knowing he was the grandson of Homu, the greatest of the head-hunting chiefs? It was worse, Rivers thought, smiling to himself, than being the great-nephew of the man who shot the man who shot Lord Nelson.

None of these questions could be pursued. It was not lack of words merely, but a lack of shared concepts. The islanders seemed hardly to have discovered the idea of personality, in the western sense, much less to have contracted the habit of introspection. Njiru was one of the most powerful men on the island, perhaps the most powerful. To Rivers and Hocart it seemed abundantly apparent that he owed his position to quite exceptional intelligence, vigour and resolution, but such qualities were never mentioned by the islanders when they attempted to explain his position. His power was attributed entirely to the number of spirits he controlled. He 'knew' Mateana. And above all, he 'knew' Ave. *Njiru knows Ave*. One of the first things he'd been told, though he hadn't understood the significance of the statement then, and perhaps did not fully understand it even now.

In view of that chink of blade on blade, what accounted for this sudden change of attitude? He was reasonably certain it was Njiru who'd put Ngea's axe in the tent. He hadn't even pretended surprise when Rivers offered it to him. And yet here he was, being apparently helpful and co-operative, actually inviting him to be present at an important ritual occasion. But then he was like this, one moment clamming up completely, even ordering other people to withhold information, and yet at other times easily the best informant on the island. Standing over them sometimes to make sure they got every detail of a ritual, every word of a prayer *exactly* right.

The inconsistency probably reflected Njiru's doubts about the reality of his own power. Others were persuaded by it, but he was capable of standing back and asking himself the hard questions. Why, if he controlled the spirits, why, if the rituals did everything he claimed for them, were the white men still here? Not Rivers and Hocart, whom he liked and respected, but the others: the government that forbade the taking of heads though the people lived for it, the traders who cheated them, the plantation bosses who exploited them, and, most of all, the missionaries who destroyed their faith. If you can't prevent such things happening, what is the actual value of your knowledge?

And so he swayed to and fro: sometimes guarding his knowledge jealously, sometimes sharing it freely, sometimes spitting it out with a bitter, angry pride, sometimes almost with gratitude to Rivers, whose obvious interest in what he was being told seemed to confirm its value. And then again he would sheer off, ashamed of ever needing that confirmation.

A stormy relationship, then, on Njiru's side, and yet the mutual respect went deep. He wouldn't kill me, Rivers thought. Then he thought, Actually, in certain circumstances, that's exactly what he'd do.

By the time they reached the turning off the coastal path, the sun was at its highest point. Sweat tickled the tip of Rivers's nose, producing a constant frenzy of irritation. His groin was a swamp. At first the darkness under the trees was welcome, after the dreadful white glare, but then a cloud of stinging insects fastened on the sweat.

Abruptly, they came out into a clearing, sharp blades of sunlight slanting down between the trees, and ahead of them, rising steeply up the slope, six or seven skull houses, their gratings ornamented with strings of dangling shells. The feeling of being watched that skulls always gave you. Dazzled by the sudden light, he followed Njiru up the slope, towards a knot of shadows, and then one of the shadows moved, resolving itself into the shape of Nareti, the blind mortuary priest who squatted there, all pointed knees and elbows, snails' trails of pus running from the corners of his eyes.

The furthest of the skull houses was being repaired, and its occupants had been taken out and arranged on the ground so that, at first sight, the clearing seemed to be cobbled with skulls. He hung back, not sure how close he was permitted to approach, and at that moment a sudden fierce gust of wind shook the trees and all the strings of votary shells rattled and clicked together.

Njiru beckoned Rivers to join him and, without further preliminary, began the prayer of purification, rubbing leaves down Nareti's legs from buttock to ankle.

'I purify at the great stream of Mondo. It flows down, it flows up, it washes away the poisonous water of the chiefly dead. The thatch is poisonous, the rafters are poisonous, the creepers are poisonous, the ground is poisonous . . .'

Among the skulls laid out on the ground were several that had belonged to children. Children loved and wept over? Or children brought back from Ysabel and Choiseul and sacrificed?

'Let me purify this priest. Let him come down and pass under. Let him come down and step over. Let him not waste away, let him not get the rash, let him not get the itch. Let him be bonito in the sea, porpoise in the sea, eel in the fresh water, crayfish in the fresh water, *vape* in the fresh water. I purify, I purify, I purify with all the chiefs.'

Njiru's voice, which had risen in pitch, dropped on the final words.

Always in Melanesia, the abrupt transition from ritual to everyday life. Njiru was soon chatting and laughing with Nareti, then he summoned Rivers to follow him. A short path led to Nareti's hut and there, squatting in the dust, having the remains of lunch licked off his face by a dog, was the small boy whom Lembu had brought from Ysabel. Healthy, well-fed. Unbruised, Rivers saw, looking closely, not happy, but then that was hardly to be hoped for. He watched him for a few minutes. At least the dog was a friend.

He was to assist Nareti, Njiru said. When he grew up he would be a mortuary priest in his turn. An odd fate, to spend one's life tending the skulls of a foreign people, but at least he would *have* a life, and perhaps not a bad one, for the mortuary priests became wealthy and enjoyed considerable respect. This taking of captives had been the custom even in the days of head-hunting, Njiru explained. He was in one of his communicative phases. Some of the 'heads' taken on a raid were always brought back alive, and kept for occasions when they might be quickly needed. A sort of living larder of heads. Such captives were never ill-treated – the idea of deliberate cruelty was foreign to the people – and indeed they often attained positions of wealth and honour, though always knowing that, at any moment, their heads might be required.

On their way back across the clearing Njiru stopped, selected the central skull from the middle row, and held it out to Rivers.

'Homu.'

Rivers took the skull, aware of the immense honour that was being done to him, and searching for something to say and the words to say it in. He ran his fingers round the occiput and traced the cranial sutures. He remembered a time at Bart's, holding a human brain in his hands for the first time, being amazed at the weight of it. This blown eggshell had contained the only product of the forces of evolution capable of understanding its own origins. But then for Njiru too the skull was sacred not in or of itself, but because it had contained the spirit, the *tomate*.

He looked at Njiru and realized it wasn't necessary

to say anything. He handed the skull back, with a slight inclination of his head, and for a moment their linked hands grasped it, each holding the object of highest value in the world.

The bullet caused gross damage to the left eye as it passed backwards in the direction of the temporal lobe. Left pupil fixed, cornea insensitive, eyelid droops, no movement of the globe except downwards. Eye blind because of rupture of the choroid and atrophy of the optic nerve. Yes. *A tendency to clonus at the right ankle joint . . .* All right.

Switching off the lighted screen and replacing the notes in the file, Rivers glanced at the cover and noticed that Hallet was in the 2nd Manchesters. He wondered if he knew Billy Prior, or whether, if he did, he would remember.

SEVENTEEN

19 October 1918

Marched all day through utter devastation. Dead horses, unburied men, stench of corruption. Sometimes you look at all this, craters, stinking mud, stagnant water, trees like gigantic burnt matches, and you think the land can't possibly recover. It's *poisoned*. Poison's dripped into it from rotting men, dead horses, gas. It will, of course. Fifty years from now a farmer'll be ploughing these fields and turn up skulls.

A huge crow flew over us, flapping and croaking mournfully. One for sorrow. The men didn't rest till they'd succeeded in spotting another.

Joy awaits us, then.

The unburied dead, though not cheerful companions for a march, had one good result. A boot for Wilson. Getting it wasn't pleasant, but once the debris left by the previous owner (*of* the previous owner) had been cleaned out it did well enough. He looks happier.

Men very cheerful for the most part, a long singing

column winding tirelessly along (but we've a long way to go yet!). I found myself thinking about Longstaffe. Not dead three weeks, and yet he rarely crosses my mind. In Tite Street, three doors down from Beattie's shop, there was an old couple who'd been married over fifty years and everybody thought when one of them went the other would be devastated. But when the husband died the old lady didn't seem all that upset, and hardly talked about him once the funeral was over. In spite of all the young male vigour around here – and my God it's bloody overwhelming at times – we're all in the same position as that old woman. Too close to death ourselves to make a fuss. We economize on grief.

Later

Men bivouac in the open, but the officers are in dugouts, the remains of an elaborate German system. The dug-outs are boarded off, but behind the planks are tunnels which reach back very deep. You can put your eye to a gap in the boards and look into darkness and after a while the eyeball begins to ache from the cold air. The extraordinary thing is everybody's slightly nervous about these tunnels, far more than about the guns that rumble and flicker and light up the sky as I write. And it's not a rational fear. It's something to do with the children whom the Pied Piper led into the mountain, who never came out again, or Rip Van Winkle who came out and found that years and years had passed and nobody knew him. It's interesting, well, at least it interests me, that we're still afraid in this irrational way when at the same time we're surrounded by the worst the twentieth century can do: shells, revolvers, rifles, guns, gas. I think it's because it strikes a particular chord. Children do go into the mountain and not come back. We've all been home on leave and found home so foreign that we couldn't fit in. What about after the war? But perhaps it's better not to think about that. Tempting fate. Anyway, here comes dinner. I'm hungry.

20 October

Another mammoth march. Lousy rotten stinking job too, rounding up the stragglers. Forget leadership. This is where leadership ends and bullying starts. I heard myself hassling and chivvying like one of those bloody instructors at Étaples. Except at least I'm *doing* what I'm bullying other people into doing.

I turned on one man, mouth open to give him a really good blast, and then I saw his face. He was asthmatic. That tight, pale, drawn worried look. If you're asthmatic yourself you can't miss it. He might as well have been carrying a placard. I fell in beside him and tried to talk to him, but he couldn't talk and march at once, or creep rather – he certainly wasn't marching. That's the thing about asthma: it creates the instant brotherhood shared humanity routinely fails to create. I got him into the horse ambulance, well propped up, gripped his wrist and said goodbye. I doubt if he saw me go. When you're as bad as that nothing matters except the next breath.

The curious thing is as soon as I saw his face, my own chest tightened, just because I'd been reminded of the possibility, I suppose. So far, touch wood, there's been no trouble. But I'm a bit wheezy tonight.

Singing very ragged by mid-afternoon, a lot of men marching in silence, it had become a test of endurance. But then suddenly, or so it seemed — we'd been marching half asleep — we found ourselves with green fields on either side, farmhouses with roofs on, trees with branches, and civilians. We'd marched right through the battlefields into what used to be securely German-held territory. Women. Children. Dogs. Cats. I think we were all amazed that the world had such creatures in it. A lot of wolf whistling at the girls, and nobody inclined to be fussy. 'Girl' soon stretched from fourteen to fifty.

I'm writing this at a kitchen table in a cottage. Outside is a farmyard with ordinary farmyard noises. Honking geese are a miracle. Though we move on again soon. They're questioning civilians in the next room, Owen's French coming in handy. And at this table, until a few weeks ago, a German officer sat and wrote letters home.

22 October

Still here, but not for much longer. We move on again later today. Not even the pouring rain that puckers the surface of the pond – with its official ducks and unofficial moorhens – can remove the feeling of serenity I have. Chest a lot easier, in spite of the damp.

24 October

More marching. I have visions of us marching into Berlin at this rate. Nearest village was shelled last night. Five civilians killed. When did we stop thinking of civilians as human? Quite a long time ago, I think. Anyhow, nobody's devastated by the news. And yet the people round here are friendly, we get on well with them. Only there's a slight wariness, I suppose. They hated the invasion, nobody doubts that, but the Germans were here a long time. An accommodation of some sort was reached. And the German troops in this area anyway seem to have been very disciplined. No atrocities. The respectable young ladies of the village are very respectable young ladies indeed, despite having spent four years in the clutches of the brutal and lascivious Hun. And the shell-holes that lie in the orchards, fields and roads round here – great gaping wounds – were made by *our* guns. The bombardment was very heavy at times. Some of the children run away from us. And yet we're greeted everywhere with open arms.

Still can't get used to ordinary noises, especially women's and children's voices. It must feel like this coming out of prison.

25 October

Owen is to be court-martialled. Mainly because he speaks French better than anybody else and all the local girls make a bee-line for him, not just thanking him either, but actually *kissing* him. I caught his eye while all this was going on, and thought I detected an answering gleam. Of irony or whatever. Anyway the Great Unkissed are thoroughly fed up with him and have convened a subalterns' court martial. Shot at dawn, I shouldn't wonder.

Wyatt, meanwhile, is visiting a farmhouse on the outskirts of the village where lives an accommodating widow and her equally accommodating but rather more nubile daughters. At this very moment, probably, he's dipping his wick where many a German wick has dipped before it. (A *frisson* wasted on Wyatt, believe me.)

But this morning I saw a woman in the village with sunlight on her hair and one of those long loaves of bread in her arms and there was more sensuality in that moment than in all Wyatt's

humping and pumping. Out of bounds, of course.
Perfectly respectable housewife doing the shopping.

26 October

This morning I went to one of the local farms to sort
out a billeting problem. The woman who runs the
farm had accused some of the men in 'C' company of
stealing eggs. They denied it vociferously, but I'm
sure she's right. After calming her down and paying
her more for the eggs than they were worth, I noticed
a boy with red hair staring at me. Not staring exactly,
but his eyes met mine longer than was strictly necessary. About sixteen, I suppose. Perhaps a bit older. He
was walking across the yard clanking a bucket of pig
swill, and after I'd taken leave of Madame (his mother,
I *think*) I followed him into the fetid darkness, full of
snuffling and munching, pigs rooting round with
moist quivering nostrils, trotting towards him on
delicate pink feet. After he poured the swill in they
squealed and guzzled for a bit, then raised their heads,
watching us calmly from under long fine white
eyelashes as they munched. I scratched their backs and
tried to talk to him. Chinks of sunlight came in
through gaps in the tiles, a smelly greenish wetness
under foot. He spoke rapidly and I got very little of it
– schoolboy French no use at all. I spun back-scratch-
ing out as long as I could, then departed, wondering
how much of that initial look I'd imagined.

Nothing particularly attractive about him – dead white skin, splodgy freckles, curious flat golden brown eyes – not that it bothered me. After two months without sex I'd have settled for the pigs.

I met him again later, near the church. There's a lane runs past the churchyard, a low stone wall on one side, a canal on the other, one of the many canals that run through this area. A rather dank gloomy stretch of water, listlessly reflecting a dense white sky, fringed by willows with limp yellow leaves. He was sitting with his big, red, raw-knuckled hands clasped between his knees. The red hair glowed in the greyish light, not bright red, not auburn, a dark, flat, burnt-looking colour.

He was very obviously lingering. He greeted me with a smile and tapped his mouth, making smoking movements. I gave him a Woodbine and stood by the canal, a few feet away, looking up and down to make sure we weren't being observed. He made smoking movements again and pointed to the packet. When I didn't immediately respond, he pointed again and said something *in German*. I thought, My God. Have you really got your head stuck so deep in the fucking pig bucket you don't know which army's up the other end? I suppose it should have disgusted me, but it didn't. In fact it had the opposite effect – I'd have given him every packet I possessed. I handed them over and he got up and led me into the trees. It took a while finding somewhere sufficiently screened. I showed him what I wanted. He leant against the tree

247

trunk, bracing himself on his hands. I pulled down his trousers and drawers and started nosing and tonguing round his arse, worrying at the crack to get in because the position hardened the muscles. A smell of chrysanths left too long in water, then a deeper friendlier smell, prim, pursed hole glistening with spit and, on the other side of that tight French sphincter, German spunk. Not literally – they left a bit longer ago than *that* – but *there* nevertheless, the shadowy figures one used to glimpse through periscopes in the trenches, and my tongue reaching out for them. I thought,

> Oh ye millions I embrace you,
> This kiss is for the whole world . . .

Suddenly it struck me as funny, and my breath made a farting noise between his buttocks and he tried to pull away, but I held on, and fucked him, and then turned him round and sucked off his quite small stubby very purple cock.

And then we parted. And I've been neurotically running my tongue round my lips feeling for sores ever since.

27 October

Everybody finds these marches gruelling. I spend a lot of my time on foot inspections. Some of the men have blisters the size of eggs. And my own feet, which were not good this morning, are now *very* not good.

But we're in decent billets tonight. I've actually got a bed in a room with roses on the wallpaper, and a few left in the garden too. Went out and picked some and put them in a bowl on the kitchen table in memory of Amiens. Big blowsy roses well past their best, but we move on again today so I won't be here to see the petals fall.

29 October

Arrived here under cover of darkness. Village wretched, people unsmiling, dazed-looking, not surprising when you think we were bombing them to buggery not long ago.

There's a rumour going round that the Austrians have signed a peace treaty. The men cheered up when they heard it, and they need cheering when you look at their feet. Nobody here can understand why it's still going on.

I lay in bed last night and listened to them in the barn singing. I wish I didn't feel they're being sacrificed to the subclauses and the small print. But I think they are.

Thursday, 31 October

And here for a while we shall stay. The Germans are dug in on the other side of the Sambre-Oise Canal, and seem to be preparing to make a stand.

The village is still occupied, but houses in the forward area have been evacuated and we're crammed into the cellar of one of them. Now and then we venture upstairs into the furnished rooms, feeling like rats or mice, and then we scurry back into our hole again. But it's warm, it *feels* safe, though the whole house shakes with the impact of exploding shells, and it's not good to think what a direct hit would do. Above ground the Germans have chopped down all the trees, but there's a great tangle of undergrowth, brambles that catch at your legs as you walk past, dead bracken the exact shade, or one of the shades, of Sarah's hair. No possibility of exercises or drill or anything. We lie low by day, and patrol at night, for of course they've left alarm posts on this side of the canal, a sort of human trip-wire to warn of an impending attack. Cleaning them out's a nasty job since it has to be silent. Knives and knobkerries in other words.

1 November

My turn to go out last night. One alarm post 'exterminated'. I hope it's the last. We crawled almost to the edge of the canal, and lay looking at it. There was just enough starlight to see by. A strong sense of the Germans on the other side, peering into the darkness as we were, silent, watchful. I had the sense that somewhere out there was a pair of eyes looking directly into mine.

The canal's raised about four feet above the surrounding fields, with drainage ditches on either side (the Germans have very sensibly flooded them). It's forty feet wide. Too wide to be easily bridged, too narrow from the point of view of a successful bombardment. There's no safety margin to allow for shells falling short, so men and equipment will have to be kept quite a long way back. Which means that when the barrage lifts, as it's supposed to do, and sweeps forward three hundred yards, there'll be about five minutes in which to get across the swampy fields, across the drainage ditches, and reach even our side of the canal. Plenty of time for them to get their breath and man the guns – though officially, of course, they'll all have been wiped out.

The field opposite's partially flooded already, and it's still raining. Not just rain, they've also flooded the drainage ditches on *their* side. From the canal the ground rises steeply to La Motte Farm, which is our objective in the attack. Uphill all the way. Not a scrap of cover. Machine-gunners behind every clump of grass.

Looking at the ground, even like that in semi-darkness, the problem became dreadfully apparent. Far clearer than it is on any of the maps, though we spend hours of every day bent over them. There are two possibilities. Either you bombard the opposite bank so heavily that no machine-gunner can possibly survive, in which case the ditches and quite possibly even the canal bank will burst, and the field on the other side will become a nightmare of weltering mud ten feet deep, as bad as anything at Passchendaele. *Or* you keep the bombardment light, move it on quickly, and wait for the infantry to catch up. In that case you take the risk that unscathed machine-gunners will pop up all over the place, and settle down for a nice bit of concentrated target practice.

It's a choice between Passchendaele and the Somme. Only a *miniature* version of each, but then that's not much consolation. It only takes one bullet per man.

They've chosen the Somme. This afternoon we had a joint briefing with the Lancashire Fusiliers on our left. Marshall-of-the-Ten-Wounds was there, surprisingly outspoken I thought, though you can afford to be when you're so covered in wound stripes and medals it's starting to look like an eccentric form of camouflage. He said his men stand *no* chance of getting up the slope with machine-guns still intact above them and no cover. Building a bridge in the open under the sort of fire we're likely to encounter is *impossible*. The whole operation's *insane*. The chances of success are *zero*.

Nobody argued with him, I mean nobody discussed it. We were just told flatly, a simple, unsupported assertion, that the weight of the artillery would overcome all opposition. I think those words sent a chill down the spine of every man there who remembered the Somme. Marshall threw his pencil down and sat with his arms folded, silent, for the rest of the briefing.

So here we sit writing letters. Supplies take a long time to get here, because the Germans blocked the roads and blew up the bridges as they withdrew.

Nobody's been inside a proper shop for six weeks, so I keep tearing pages out of the back of this book and giving them to people.

Not many left now. But enough.

2 November 1918   2nd Manchester Regt. France

My dear Rivers,

As you'll have realized from my last letter, I'm still intact. Should this happy state of affairs not continue, I would be grateful if you would try to see my mother. She took quite a fancy to you when you met last year at Craiglockhart and you, more than most people, would know what to say. Or have the sense to say nothing, which was always rather your forte, wasn't it?

My nerves are in perfect working order. By which I mean that in my present situation the only sane thing to do is to run away, and I will not do it. Test passed?

Yours

Billy Prior

A chilly little note to send to someone who's done so much for me. Wrong tone completely, but there isn't time to get it right.

I daren't think about Sarah.

3 November

We're packed so tight in this cellar my elbow's constantly being jogged by people on either side. Cigarette smoke stings my eyes, I honestly believe if you ran out of fags here you'd just need to breathe deeply. But I've got enough to last, even after my spasm of generosity on the canal bank. Which this morning I reread, tore out and burned. Another canal bank meeting awaits – but this time the sort people approve of.

Curious day – it seems to have gone on for ever. We had another briefing at a farmhouse further along the lane. We were greeted by a little yapping terrier, still a puppy, black and white and full of himself, tucking one of his legs up as he ran so that at first I thought he was crippled, but the children in the house said no, he always runs like that. He quietened down a bit, but then got excited and started yapping again. Winterton nodded at me, and said, 'We can't have that.'

I shot it myself. I'm proud of that. In the trenches sometimes you'd be watching through a periscope and you'd see a German soldier – generally well back in the support lines – walking along believing himself to be safe, and he'd drop his breeches and settle down for a nice contented crap. You don't want to shoot him because there's something about the vulnerability of that bare arse, you feel the draught up your own crack, a moment of basic human empathy. So you point him out to the sentry and order the sentry to shoot him. That lets everybody off the hook – you haven't shot him, the sentry has, but only under orders.

But I shot the dog myself. I took him into the barn holding on to his collar. He knew something bad was going to happen, and he rolled over on to his back and showed me his puppy-pink tummy and widdled a bit, quite certain these devices for deflecting aggression would work. I tickled him behind his ear and said, 'Sorry, old son. I'm human – we're not like that.'

And I'm glad of the fug of human warmth in here, and not just because it keeps out the wind and rain. Those who've bagged themselves seats by the fire have steam rising from their boots and puttees. The rest of us just wiggle our toes and make do.

Having said I daren't think about Sarah, I think about her all the time. I remember the first time we met – that ludicrous wrestling match on a tombstone which in retrospect seems a rather appropriate start for a relationship so hedged in by death. And before that in the pub, plying her with port to get her knickers off, and she wanted to talk about Johnny's death and I didn't want to listen. Loos, she said. I remember standing by the bar and thinking that words didn't mean anything any more. Patriotism honour courage vomit vomit vomit. Only the names meant anything. Mons, Loos, the Somme, Arras, Verdun, Ypres.

But now I look round this cellar with the candles burning on the tables and our linked shadows leaping on the walls, and I realize there's another group of words that still mean something. Little words that trip through sentences unregarded: us, them, we, they, here, there. These are the words of power, and long after we're gone, they'll lie about in the language, like the unexploded grenades in these fields, and any one of them'll take your hand off.

Wyatt sleeps like a baby, except that no baby ever snored like that. Hoggart's peeling potatoes. Mugs of chlorine-tasting tea stand round. And somebody's chopping wood and feeding it to the fire, though it's so damp every fresh stick produces darkness, sizzling, a temporary shadowing of faces and eyes and then the flames lick round it, and the fire blazes up again. We need a good fire. Everybody's coughing and wheezing, a nasty cold going the rounds. I'm starting to feel a tickle in my throat, hot and shivery at the same time. I think of rats on the canal bank with long naked tails and the thought of that cold water is definitely not inviting. But we sing, we tell jokes and every joke told here is funny. Everybody's amazingly cheerful. The word I'm trying not to use is fey. There *is* an element of that. We all know what the chances are.

And soon I shall turf Wyatt out of that bunk and try to get some sleep.

Five months ago Charles Manning offered me a job at the Ministry of Munitions and I turned it down, and said if I was sent back to France . . . 'If if if if – I shall sit in a dug-out and look back to this afternoon, and I shall think, "You *bloody* fool." '

I remember sitting on the stiff brocade sofa in his drawing-room as I said it.

Well, here I am, in what passes for a dug-out. And I look round me at all these faces and all I can think is: What an utter bloody fool I would have been not to come back.

EIGHTEEN

Brown fog enveloped the hospital. Coils of sulphurous vapour hung in the entrance hall, static, whirled into different patterns whenever somebody entered or left the building. He'd gone out himself earlier in the evening to buy a paper from the stand outside Victoria Station, a brisk ten-minute walk there and back, a chance to get some air into his lungs, though air these days scorched the throat. The news was good. At any moment now, one felt, the guns would stop and they would all be released into their private lives. They all felt it – and yet it almost seemed not to matter. The end that everybody had longed for was overshadowed by the Spanish influenza epidemic that had the hospital in its grip. If somebody had rushed along the corridor now opening doors and shouting, 'The war's over,' he'd have said, 'Oh, really?' and gone back to writing up notes.

He looked at his watch and stood up. Time to go up to the ward.

Marsden was trying to catch his eye. He'd had the impression that morning, during his ward round, that Marsden wanted to ask something, but had been deterred by the formality of the occasion. Rivers had a quick word with Sister Roberts – the staffing situation for this duty was particularly bad – and then went and sat by Marsden's bed, chatting about this and that while he worked himself up to say whatever it was he wanted to say. It was quite simple. He'd overheard a junior doctor talking to a colleague at the foot of his bed and had caught the phrase 'elicited the coital reflex'. Did this mean, Marsden wanted to know, that he would *eventually*, he stressed, hedging his bets, not *now* obviously, *eventually*, be able to have sex again? 'Have sex' was produced in a flat, no nonsense, all-chaps-together tone. He meant 'make love'. He meant 'have children'. His wife's photograph stood on his locker. Rivers's neck muscles tensed with the effort of not looking at it. No, he said slowly, it didn't mean that. He explained what it meant. Marsden wasn't listening, but he needed a smoke-screen of words behind which to prepare his reaction. He was pleating the hem of the sheet between his fingertips. 'Well,' he said casually, when Rivers had finished. 'I didn't really think it meant that. Just thought I'd ask.'

One incident; one day.

Faces shadowed by steel helmets, they would hardly have recognized each other, even if the faint starlight had enabled them to see clearly. Prior, crouching in a ditch beside the crossroads, kept looking at the inside of his left wrist where normally his watch would have been. It had been taken away from him twenty minutes ago to be synchronized. The usual symptoms: dry mouth, sweaty palms, pounding heart, irritable bladder, cold feet. What a brutally accurate term 'cold feet' was. Though 'shitting yourself' – the other brutally accurate term – did *not* apply. He'd been glugging Tincture of Opium all day, as had several others of the old hands. He'd be shitting bricks for a fortnight when this was over, but at least he wouldn't be shitting himself tonight.

He looked again at his wrist, caught Owen doing the same, smiled with shared irritation, said nothing. He stared at the stars, trying to locate the plough, but couldn't concentrate. Rain clouds were massing. All we need. A few minutes later a runner came back with his watch and with a tremendous sense – delusional, of course – of being in control again he strapped it on.

Then they were moving forward, hundreds of men eerily quiet, starlit shadows barely darkening the grass. And no dogs barked.

The clock at the end of the ward blurred, then moved into focus again. He was finding it difficult to keep awake now that the rounds were done, the reports written and his task was simply to *be there*, ready for whatever emergencies the night might throw his way. Sister Roberts put a mug of orange-coloured tea, syrupy with sugar, in front of him, and he took a gulp. They sat together at the night nurses' station – there were no night nurses, they were all off with flu – drinking the too strong, too sweet tea, watching the other end of the ward, where the green screens had been placed round Hallet's bed. A single lamp shone above his bed so the green curtains glowed against the darkness of the rest of the ward. Through a gap between the screens Rivers could see one of the family, a young boy, fourteen, fifteen years old perhaps, Hallet's younger brother, wriggling about on his chair, bored with the long hours of waiting and knowing it was unforgivable to be bored.

'I wish the mother would go home and lie down,' Sister Roberts said. 'She's absolutely at the end of her tether.' A sniff. 'And that girl looks the hysterical type to me.'

She never liked the girls. 'Is she his sister?'

'Fiancée.'

A muttering from behind the screen, but no discernible words. Rivers stood up. 'I'd better have a look.'

'Do you want the relatives out?'

'Please. It'll only take a minute.'

The family looked up as he pushed the screens aside. They had been sitting round this bed off and on for nearly thirty-six hours, ever since Hallet's condition had begun to deteriorate. Mrs Hallet, the mother, was on Hallet's right, he suspected because

262

the family had decided she should be spared, as far as possible, seeing the left side of Hallet's face. The worst was hidden by the dressing over the eye, but still enough was visible. The father sat on the bad side, a middle-aged man, very erect, retired professional army, in uniform for the duration of the war. He had a way of straightening his shoulders, bracing himself that suggested chronic back pain rather than a reaction to the present situation. And then the girl, whose name was . . . Susan, was it? She sat, twisting a handkerchief between her fingers, often with a polite, meaningless smile on her face, in the middle of the family she had been going to join and must now surely realize she would not be joining. And the boy, who was almost the most touching of all, gauche, graceless, angry with everything, his voice sometimes squeaking humiliatingly so that he blushed, at other times braying down the ward, difficult, rebellious, demanding attention, because he was afraid if he stopped behaving like this he would cry.

They stood up when he came in, looking at him in a way familiar from his earliest days in hospital medicine. They expected him to *do* something. Although they'd been told Hallet was critically ill, they were still hoping he'd 'make him better'.

Sister Roberts asked them to wait outside and they retreated to the waiting-room at the end of the main corridor.

He looked at Hallet. The whole of the left side of

his face drooped. The exposed eye was sunk deep in his skull, open, though he didn't seem to be fully conscious. His hair had been shaved off, preparatory to whatever operation had left the horseshoe-shaped scar, now healing ironically well, above the suppurating wound left by the rifle bullet. The hernia cerebri pulsated, looking like some strange submarine form of life, the mouth of a sea anemone perhaps. The whole of the left side of his body was useless. Even when he was conscious enough to speak the drooping of the mouth and the damage to the lower jaw made his speech impossible to follow. This, more than anything else, horrified his family. You saw them straining to understand, but they couldn't grasp a word he said. His voice came in a whisper because he lacked the strength to project it. He seemed to be whispering now. Rivers bent over him, listened, then straightened up, deciding he must have imagined the sound. Hallet had not stirred, beyond the usual twitching below the coverlet, the constant clonus to which his right ankle joint was subject.

Why are you alive? Rivers thought, looking down into the gargoyled face.

Mate, would have been Njiru's word for this: the state of which death is the appropriate and therefore the desirable outcome. He would have seen Hallet as being, in every meaningful way, dead already, and his sole purpose would have been to hasten the moment of actual death: *mate ndapu*, die finish. Rivers fingered his lapel badge, his unimpaired nerves trans-

he's
say

jor
nt,
ou

ns
a

al
y
e
)

of the caduceus to his undamaged
ce to a different set of beliefs con-
he conflict ever breaking the surface

t's pulse. 'All right,' he said to Sister
an let them back in.'
her walk off, then thought it was
to face them, and followed her down
passing Mrs Hallet on the way. She
n she saw him, but the drive to get
son was too strong. Susan and the
ther followed on behind. He found
lingering by an open window, smoking
breath of muggy, damp, foggy air came
m, a reminder that there was an outside

, isn't it?' Major Hallet said, raising the
Well?'
hesitated.
ng now, eh?'
ot long.'
te of his terseness, tears immediately welled
ajor Hallet's eyes. He turned away, his voice
. 'He's been so brave. He's been so bloody
A moment during which he struggled for
l. 'How long exactly do you think?'
on't know. Hours.'
God.'
eep talking to him. He *does* recognize your
s and he can understand.'

'But we can't understand *him*. It's terrible, obviously expecting an answer and we can't anything.'

They went back to the ward together, M Hallet pausing outside the screen for a mom bracing his back. A muttering from the bed. 'Y see?' Major Hallet said helplessly.

Rivers followed him through the gap in the scre and leant over to listen to Hallet. His voice wa slurred whisper. 'Shotvarfet.'

At first Rivers could only be sure of the init consonant and thought he might be trying to s 'Susan', but the phrase was longer than that. H straightened and shook his head. 'Keep talking t him, Mrs Hallet. He does recognize your voice.'

She bent forward and shyly, covered with th social embarrassment that crops up so agonizingly or these occasions, tried to talk, telling him news or home, Auntie Ethel sent her love, Madeleine was getting married in April . . .

Susan had that smile on her lips again, fixed, meaningless, a baboon rictus of sheer terror. And the boy's face, a mask of fear and fury because he knew that any moment now the tears would start, and he'd be shamed in front of some merciless tribunal in his own mind.

Rivers left them to it. Sister Roberts and the one orderly were busy with Adams who had to be turned every hour. He sat in the night station's circle of light, looking up and down the ward, forcing himself to name and recall the details of every patient, his tired mind waiting for the next jerk of the clock.

The glowing green screens round Hallet's bed reminded him of the tent on Eddystone, on the nights when the insects were really bad and they had to take the lamp inside. You'd go out into the bush and come back and there'd be this great glow of light, and Hocart's shadow huge on the canvas. Safety, or as close to it as you could get on the edge of the dark.

On their last evening he sat outside the tent, packing cases full of clothes and equipment ranged around him, typing up his final notes. Hocart was away on the other side of the island and not due back for hours. Working so close to the light his eyes grew tired, and he sat back rubbing the inner corners; he opened them again to find Njiru a few feet away watching him, having approached silently on his bare feet.

Rivers took the lamp from the table and set it on the ground, squatting down beside it, since he knew Njiru was more comfortable on the ground. The bush exuded blackness. The big moths that loved a particular flowering bush that grew all round the tent bumped furrily against the glass, so that he and Njiru sat in a cloud of pale wings.

They chatted for a while about some of the more than four hundred acquaintances they now had in common, then a long easy silence fell.

'Kundaite says you know Ave,' Rivers said very quietly, almost as if the bush itself had spoken, and Njiru were being asked to do no more than think aloud.

Njiru said, almost exactly as he'd said at the beginning, 'Kundaite he no speak true, he savvy *gammon* 'long *nanasa*,' but now he spoke with a faint growl of laughter in his voice, adding in English, 'He is a liar.'

'He *is* a liar, but I think you do know Ave.'

He was reminded suddenly of an incident in the Torres Straits when Haddon had been trying to get skulls to measure. One man had said, with immense dignity, 'Be patient. You will have all our skulls in time.' It was not a comfortable memory. He was not asking for skulls but he was asking for something at least equally sacred. He leant forward and their shadows leapt and grappled against the bush. 'Tell me about Ave.'

Ave lives in Ysabel. He is both one spirit and many spirits. His mouth is long and filled with the blood of the men he devours. Kita and Mateana are nothing beside him because they destroy only the individual, but Ave kills 'all people 'long house'. The broken rainbow belongs to him, and presages both epidemic disease and war. Ave is the destroyer of peoples.

And the words of exorcism? He told him even that, the last bubbles rising from the mouth of a drowning man. Not only told him, but, with that blend of scholarly exactitude and intellectual impatience for which he was remarkable, insisted on Rivers learning the words in Melanesian, in the 'high speech', until he had the inflection on every syllable perfect. This was the basis, Rivers thought, toiling and stumbling over the words, of Njiru's power, the reason why on meeting him even the greatest chiefs stepped off the path.

'And now,' Njiru said, lifting his head in a mixture of pride and contempt, 'now you will put it in your book.'

I never have, Rivers thought. His and Hocart's book on Eddystone had been one of the casualties of the war, though hardly – he glanced up and down the ward with its rows of brain-damaged and paralysed young men – the most significant.

He had spoken them, though, during the course of a lecture to the Royal Society, and had been delighted to find that he didn't need to consult his notes as he spoke. He was still word-perfect.

A commotion from behind the screens. Hallet had begun to cry out and his family was trying to soothe him. A muttering all along the ward as the other patients stirred and grumbled in their sleep, dragged reluctantly back into consciousness. But the grumbling stopped as they realized where the cries were coming from. A silence fell. Faces turned towards the screens as if the battle being waged behind them was every man's battle.

Rivers walked quietly across. The family stood up again as he came in. 'No, it's all right,' he said. 'No need to move.'

He took Hallet's pulse. He felt the parents' gaze on him, the father's red-veined, unblinking eyes and the mother's pale fierce face with its working mouth.

'This is it, isn't it?' Major Hallet said in a whisper.

Rivers looked down at Hallet, who was now fully conscious. Oh God, he thought, it's going to be one of those. He shook his head. 'Not long.'

The barrage was due to start in fifteen minutes' time. Prior shared a bar of chocolate with Robson, sitting hunched up together against the damp cold mist. Then they started crawling forward. The sappers, who were burdened by materials for the construction of the pontoon bridge, were taking the lane, so the Manchesters had to advance over the waterlogged fields. The rain had stopped, but the already marshy ground had flooded in places, and over each stretch of water lay a thick blanket of mist. Concentrate on nothing but the moment, Prior told himself, moving forward on knees and elbows like a frog or a lizard or like – like anything except a man. First the right knee, then the left, then the right, then the left again, and again, and again, slithering through fleshy green grass that smelled incredibly sharp as scrabbling boots cut it. Even with all this mist there was now a perceptible thinning of the light, a gleam from the canal where it ran between spindly, dead trees.

There is to be no retirement under any circumstances.
That was the order. They have tied us to the stake,
we cannot fly, but bear-like we must fight the course.
The men were silent, staring straight ahead into the
mist. Talk, even in whispers, was forbidden. Prior
looked at his watch, licked dry lips, watched the
second hand crawl to the quarter hour. All around
him was a tension of held breath. 5.43. Two more
minutes. He crouched further down, whistle clenched
between his teeth.

Prompt as ever, hell erupted. Shells whined over,
flashes of light, plumes of water from the drainage
ditches, tons of mud and earth flung into the air. A
shell fell short. The ground shook beneath them and
a shower of pebbles and clods of earth peppered their
steel helmets. Five minutes of this, five minutes of
the air bursting in waves against your face, men with
dazed faces braced against it, as they picked up the
light bridges meant for fording the flooded drainage
ditches, and carried them out to the front. Then,
abruptly, silence. A gasp for air, then noise again, but
further back, as the barrage lifted and drummed
down on to the empty fields.

Prior blew the whistle, couldn't hear it, was on his
feet and running anyway, urging the men on with
wordless cries. They rushed forward, making for the
line of trees. Prior kept shouting, 'Steady, steady!
Not too fast on the left!' It was important there
should be no bunching when they reached the
bridges. 'Keep it straight!' Though the men were

stumbling into quagmires or tripping over clumps of grass. A shell whizzing over from the German side exploded in a shower of mud and water. And another. He saw several little figures topple over, it didn't look serious, somehow, they didn't look like beings who could be hurt.

Bridges laid down, quickly, efficiently, no bunching at the crossings, just the clump of boots on wood, and then they emerged from beneath the shelter of the trees and out into the terrifying openness of the bank. As bare as an eyeball, no cover anywhere, and the machine-gunners on the other side were alive and well. They dropped down, firing to cover the sappers as they struggled to assemble the bridge, but nothing covered *them*. Bullets fell like rain, puckering the surface of the canal, and the men started to fall. Prior saw the man next to him, a silent, surprised face, no sound, as he twirled and fell, a slash of scarlet like a huge flower bursting open on his chest. Crawling forward, he fired at the bank opposite though he could hardly see it for the clouds of smoke that drifted across. The sappers were still struggling with the bridge, binding pontoon sections together with wire that sparked in their hands as bullets struck it. And still the terrible rain fell. Only two sappers left, and then the Manchesters took over the building of the bridge. Kirk paddled out in a crate to give covering fire, was hit, hit again, this time in the face, went on firing directly at the machine-gunners who crouched in their defended holes only a few yards away. Prior was about to start across the water with ammunition when he was himself hit, though it didn't feel like a bullet, more like a blow from something big and hard, a truncheon or a cricket bat, only it knocked him off his feet and he fell, one arm trailing over the edge of the canal.

He tried to turn to crawl back beyond the drainage ditches, knowing it was only a matter of time before he was hit again, but the gas was thick here and he couldn't reach his mask. Banal, simple, repetitive thoughts ran round and round his mind. *Balls up. Bloody mad. Oh Christ.* There was no pain, more a spreading numbness that left his brain clear. He saw Kirk die. He saw Owen die, his body lifted off the ground by bullets, describing a slow arc in the air as it fell. It seemed to take for ever to fall, and Prior's consciousness fluttered down with it. He gazed at his reflection in the water, which broke and reformed and broke again as bullets hit the surface and then, gradually, as the numbness spread, he ceased to see it.

The light was growing now, the subdued, brownish light of a November dawn. At the far end of the ward, Simpson, too far gone himself to have any understanding of what was happening, jargoned and gobbled away, but all the other faces were turned towards the screens, each man lending the little strength he had to support Hallet in his struggle.

So far, except for the twice repeated whisper and

the wordless cries, Hallet had been silent, but now the whisper began again, only more loudly. *Shotvarfet. Shotvarfet.* Again and again, increasing in volume as he directed all his strength into the cry. His mother tried to soothe him, but he didn't hear her. *Shotvarfet. Shotvarfet.* Again and again, each time louder, ringing across the ward. He opened his one eye and gazed directly at Rivers, who had come from behind the screens and was standing at the foot of his bed.

'What's he saying?' Major Hallet asked.

Rivers opened his mouth to say he didn't know and then realized he did. 'He's saying, "It's not worth it."'

'Oh, it is worth it, it *is*,' Major Hallet said, gripping his son's hand. The man was in agony. He hardly knew what he was saying.

'*Shotvarfet.*'

The cry rose again as if he hadn't spoken, and now the other patients were growing restless. A buzz of protest not against the cry, but in support of it, a wordless murmur from damaged brains and drooping mouths.

'*Shotvarfet. Shotvarfet.*'

'I can't stand much more of this,' Major Hallet said. The mother's eyes never left her son's face. Her lips were moving though she made no sound. Rivers was aware of a pressure building in his own throat as that single cry from the patients went on and on. He could not afterwards be sure that he had succeeded in keeping silent, or whether he too had joined in. All he could remember later was gripping the metal rail at the end of the bed till his hands hurt.

And then suddenly it was over. The mangled words faded into silence, and a moment or two later, with an odd movement of the chest and stomach muscles like somebody taking off a too tight jumper, Hallet died.

Rivers reached the bedside before the family realized he was gone, closed the one eye, and from sheer force of habit looked at his watch.

'6. 25,' he said, addressing Sister Roberts.

He raised the sheet as far as Hallet's chin, arranged his arms by his sides and withdrew silently, leaving the family alone with their grief, wishing, as he pulled the screens more closely together, that he had not seen the young girl turn aside to hide her expression of relief.

On the edge of the canal the Manchesters lie, eyes still open, limbs not yet decently arranged, for the stretcher-bearers have departed with the last of the wounded, and the dead are left alone. The battle has withdrawn from them; the bridge they succeeded in building was destroyed by a single shell. Further down the canal another and more successful crossing is being attempted, but the cries and shouts come faintly here.

The sun has risen. The first shaft strikes the water and creeps towards them along the bank, discovering here the back of a hand, there the side of a neck, lending a rosy glow to skin from which the blood has fled, and then, finding nothing here that can respond to it, the shaft of light passes over them and begins to probe the distant fields.

Grey light tinged with rosy pink seeps in through the tall windows. Rivers, slumped at the night nurses' station, struggles to stay awake. On the edge of sleep he hears Njiru's voice, repeating the words of the exorcism of Ave.

O Sumbi! O Gesese! O Palapoko! O Gorepoko! O you Ngengere at the root of the sky. Go down, depart ye.

And there, suddenly, not separate from the ward, not in any way ghostly, not in *fashion blong tomate*, but himself in every particular, advancing down the ward of the Empire Hospital, attended by his shadowy retinue, as Rivers had so often seen him on the coastal path on Eddystone, came Njiru.

There is an end of men, an end of chiefs, an end of chieftains' wives, an end of chiefs' children – then go down and depart. Do not yearn for us, the fingerless, the crippled, the broken. Go down and depart, oh, oh, oh.

He bent over Rivers, staring into his face with those piercing hooded eyes. A long moment, and then the brown face, with its streaks of lime, faded into the light of the daytime ward.

AUTHOR'S NOTE

The reader may wish to know more about some of the historical characters encountered in this novel.

Colonel Marshall-of-the-Ten-Wounds was killed attempting to cross the Sambre-Oise canal, having led his men 'without regard for his personal safety'. He was awarded a posthumous VC.

James Kirk, who paddled himself out on to the canal to give covering fire, was also awarded a posthumous VC.

Wilfred Owen's MC, for gallantry in capturing an enemy machine-gun and inflicting 'considerable losses' on the enemy at the battle of Joncourt, was awarded after his death.

Rivers drew on his Eddystone data in several published papers, but the major joint work he and Hocart planned was never written. His notebooks are in the Rare Manuscripts Department of Cambridge University Library.

Njiru, Kundaite, Namboko Taru, Namboko

Emele, Nareti, Lembu and the captive child are also historical, but of them nothing more is known.

The following works can be unreservedly recommended:

W. H. R. Rivers by Richard Slobodin (Columbia University Press, 1978)

Memories of Lewis Carroll by Katharine Rivers, with an Introduction by Richard Slobodin (Library Research News, McMaster University, 1976)

Collected Letters of Wilfred Owen (Oxford University Press, 1967)

Wilfred Owen by Jon Stallworthy (Oxford University Press, 1974)

Owen the Poet by Dominic Hibberd (Macmillan, 1986)

Wilfred Owen, The Last Year by Dominic Hibberd (Constable, 1992)

Wilfred Owen's Voices: Language and Community by Douglas Kerr (Clarendon Press, 1993)

Wilfred Owen, Poet and Soldier by Helen McPhail (Gliddon Books in association with the Wilfred Owen Association, 1993)